About the author

Years ago I tried to write but the next day I could not read what I had written.

I gave up until a friend said, "What about your computer?"

She set up the computer.

"I cannot type."

"Type with two fingers. Sit down and start writing."

This is my first book I hope the next one is as good.

MARTY AND JONNIE

Douglas Stewart

MARTY AND JONNIE

Vanguard Press

A CIP catalogue record for this title is
available from the British Library.

ISBN 978-1-80016-087-3

Vanguard Press is an imprint of
Pegasus Elliot MacKenzie Publishers Ltd.
www.pegasuspublishers.com

First Published in 2021

Vanguard Press
Sheraton House Castle Park
Cambridge England

Printed & Bound in Great Britain

CHAPTER ONE

Early one summer morning, just before sunrise, some time in the early seventies, in the Sydney suburb of Alexandra, a tall, thin, young man was riding along the footpath in the dark on a deserted side street. There was another young man sitting on the handlebars, with his legs dangling either side of the front wheel. They were traveling rather fast in the dark with the passenger in such a precarious position.

A high brick wall ran along the inside edge of the footpath. When the bicycle came to a tree, the pedaller stopped then the passenger stood up on the handlebars and disappeared into the tree. The rider continued to the corner and hid the bicycle behind a bus shelter, then ran back along the wall to a large gate and stood in the shadows.

Meanwhile the other youth climbed up the tree and out onto a branch. He jumped onto the ledge on top of the wall and quickly moved along until he came to the edge of a building that butted against the wall. He climbed onto the gutter of the building, then quickly ran along the gutter until the building, which was a large shed, butted against the main building.

Like a monkey, the youth then slid down the drainpipe and ran to the gate. He turned off the alarm—there was a switch next to the gate—then pulled back the bolts and opened the gates. His partner was waiting outside to help him.

The youth outside ran to a truck parked in the yard and opened the driver's door. He had a long tube strapped upright on his back, which he tossed on the seat then opened it. Inside were rolls of paper. He handed the small sheets to the other youth and they then removed the thin protective backing and attached the posters over the signs on the truck. The tall one jumped into the truck, found the ignition key under the corner of the floor mat and started the truck. He quickly backed out the gate and drove off.

The other youth closed the gates from the inside and bolted them. He turned on the alarm and left by a small door in one of the gates. He ran to the corner, jumped on the bicycle and rode off.

The smaller youth could just reach the pedals while standing. He could not reach the seat. He was uncomfortable because the neck of the seat rubbed his back, so he had to lean forward to pedal. He cut through lanes and alleys and arrived at their destination at the same time the truck turned the corner. He jumped off the bike and opened a large electric overhead door. The truck drove in. The other youth took the bicycle inside and closed the door and turned on the lights.

The room was large. Years ago, it had been a garage for a taxi company. The hoist and compressor were still there. The smaller youth started the compressor while the driver began moving large heavy planks in the floor. They both struggled to move the planks. Underneath the floor was a car hoist. The truck was driven on to the hoist, then disappeared into the floor.

They replaced the planks, then swept floor dust into the cracks. They turned out the lights, went out the back door, down the lane to the street and walked home.

Jonathon Eastwood was the tall bike rider. He lived with his mother in a rented town house two blocks from the garage. He was seventeen, a third-year student at the local high school. Jonnie, as he liked to be called, was the tallest student at the school. He had thin arms and legs. His fingers were long and slim.

Jonnie did not mind being tall. He was used to others staring at him. There was nothing he could about it anyway. But he was very self-conscious about his feet. Everybody looked at his large feet at the end of his slim legs.

Jonnie was born in Queensland. His father was a train driver for the Queensland Railroad. His father and mother did not get along, and when Jonnie was eleven, he and his mother moved to Sydney and lived with his mother's brother until she found a job and could afford to rent. His uncle and aunt lived around the corner. That was where Jonnie spent most of his time.

From the moment, he was born Jonnie was a strange looking child. His fingers and toes were longer than a normal child's. He was always skinny. His father always taunted him. He accused his wife of messing around with another man, said the child was not his.

Jonnie's father would show him off to everyone he met. Just before the family broke up his father took him to the pub. He sat him on the bar and showed him off like some sort of freak to the drinkers. Jonnie was so traumatised he would not leave the house, and ran and hid every time he saw his father. It was the final straw. His mother packed up and they moved to Sydney.

Martin McAlister lived another block further along than Jonnie. Where Jonnie was tall, Marty was short, the shortest boy in the school. They met in the seventh grade when Jonnie enrolled there. Marty was small but of solid build. He was strong, quick and agile. He was the clever one of the two.

Marty was pleased when Jonnie started school. The bullies left him alone and turned on the new boy. They soon became mates because they did not make fun of each other.

The taunters had to keep at least arm's length away from Marty. He was strong, and when they got close his punch would hurt. Jonnie had a secret weapon. When someone got close to him, he would knee them. His leg moved so fast you could not see the action.

Martin lived with his parents. His father was a foreman in the car factory. His mother was a part time teacher. They were a close, happy family. While Jonnie was ridiculed by his father, Marty's parents did all they could to encourage him. Other than the teasing at school and the occasional odd stare, no one bothered him, but he was still conscious of his small stature.

Marty and Jonnie hung around together at school. Their friendship evolved with time. Soon they walked to school together and hung around after school and on weekends.

Jonnie was tall with long legs. Mary could not keep up to him but Jonnie could not run. He would trip over his big feet when he tried. Marty's legs were short so he could not run any faster than Jonnie could walk.

They had bicycles but the same thing occurred. With his long legs, Jonnie could keep up with the fastest rider, but Marty had a small sized one speed bike. No matter how fast he pumped, he could not keep up with Jonnie. They were nearly equal on skateboards, but Mary had to pump three times to Jonnie's once. One long push with his long leg and Jonnie would be off and away.

Neither of them were very good at sports. Jonnie could not run or catch a ball. The only thing Marty was good at was gymnastics. They taught themselves simple moves on a pipe they set up in Jonnie's backyard.

They got their ideas from videos. Their favourite was trick riding on bicycles. Many hours were spent riding around the yard or training on the trapeze.

The boys were restricted in what they could do because they did not have any money to buy the expensive bicycles and skateboards needed for their tricks. The only work they could do was cutting their own lawns. Jonnie would push the lawnmower and Marty would sweep and rake.

Marty picked up a broken three speed bicycle and put the three-speed hub on his small wheel so he could keep up to Jonnie. It worked fine, but the brakes did not work well at the faster speed.

As time went by, they were pleased with what they could do.

Marty and Jonnie roamed around a lot at night. During the day they practiced in their back yard and used the skateboard ramp and did tricks on their bikes at night when no one was around.

Their lives changed when they saw a video on street gymnastics.

The back yard was converted into an obstacle course. Soon they were jumping over hurdles and running along a narrow plank. They could do flips and jump and roll. One of their favourite tricks was for Marty to run at Jonnie, jump and put his foot in Jonnie's clasped hands. Jonnie would catapult him high in the air. The other one was running up a wall and flipping over backwards.

They made harnesses to strap their skateboards to their backs so they could quickly travel almost anywhere, either on their bikes, skateboards or climbing around.

Money was their only problem. Their equipment was not strong enough to take the strain of their tricks. They snapped many a skateboard in half. The bicycles would break under the strain. They tried to build their own bikes but they were awkward and heavy. They did the best they could with what they had.

CHAPTER TWO

The boys were sixteen, in their second year of high school. The other students did not make fun of them, but they felt awkward around them, so they did not have many friends and kept to themselves.

All students had to do physical education, but Marty and Jonnie would sit and watch the others.

One afternoon the class was playing basketball. The coach also taught the school team and would chastise Jonnie for not playing. He was the tallest one in the school and should be on the team. Many times Jonnie explained to the coach that he could not run up and down the court. That day the coach made Jonnie get out on the court and play. Of course, he did not do very well, so the coach began criticizing him in front of his classmates, trying to shame him into playing for the school.

The coach walked away, leaving Jonnie in the centre of the court. He called to Jonnie to toss the ball to him. Jonnie held the basketball in his left hand and flipped it with his right hand across the court through the basket without touching the sides. The coach just stared. When he turned to speak to Jonnie was gone.

That evening he knocked on Jonnie's door and apologised.

"The team needs you," he pleaded. "There are not many good players on the team."

"I will play only on my terms," Jonnie said. "I will not run up and down the court. I will stay in the centre and toss baskets or play defence."

Jonnie soon became the star player when they started winning games.

Late one afternoon when Jonnie was practicing basketball, Marty was at the video shop looking around. He was in the rear where the cheap weekly videos were when two men came in and bailed up the proprietor. A few angry words were said then the proprietor handed them some money and they left.

Marty was upset at what he saw so he followed the two men on his skateboard. They drove a short distance then turned down a lane into a parking bay and went into a back door of a café. Marty climbed into a tree to look around. He saw the man though a window on the upper floor.

The man opened a closet, took out a steel box, then reached behind a box on a shelf for a key. He opened the box and put the money he took from the video shop in the box. He locked it then put it away. Soon the men appeared out the rear door then the two of them drove off. Marty waited for a bit, then jumped out of the tree and ran across the street. He jumped on the fence and ran across the top of it to the shed next to the building.

He was up on the shed roof and in through the window in a flash. He retrieved the box, opened it, took all the money and put it back. He was in and out of the room in less than two minutes and away on his skateboard.

Marty was practising in the back yard when Jonnie came home. When he saw the grin on Marty's face he had to ask, "What have you been up to now?"

"Come inside, I'll show you."

Jonnie was sitting on his bed. He said, "Well, come on, tell me what's going on."

Marty reached in his inner jacket pocket and tossed a handful of notes on to the bed. Jonnie just stared. His friend tossed another hand full then said, "Our money problems are over. We can do what we want now."

Jonnie sat there with his mouth open staring at the money. Finally he said, "Where did you get all this money?"

"I stole it, how else could I get that much money?"

"Are you crazy? We'll end up in jail."

"Relax, no one will ever know about it."

Marty told how he got the money. Jonnie was relieved and said, "Those thugs stole the money so they deserve what they got. Now we can buy the things we always wanted."

"We'll have to be careful. How will we explain where the money came from?" Marty asked.

"We should give some of it to Sam at the video shop," Jonnie said. "He can't afford to give it to crooks. How much is there?"

"I don't know, let's count it."

"Wow!" Jonnie exclaimed, "two thousand two hundred. We're rich."

"We'll give two hundred to Sam," Marty said. "We can do it now."

There were a few people in the shop, so Jonnie reached over to Sam's jacket when he was busy and slipped an envelope in a sleeve. They browsed and borrowed two videos, then left.

"I feel good," Jonnie said. "I know how Robin Hood must have felt, robbing the rich and giving it to the poor."

"I wonder what will happen when the crooks find out their money is gone.?" Marty said.

On Saturday morning the boys walked to the sports store. It was a long walk but they didn't mind; they were going to ride back on their new bikes.

The proprietor knew them because they often bought parts from him.

"Good morning, boys, what are you looking for today?"

"We're learning to do trick riding," Marty said. "Do you have a trick bike?"

"They're over there, but they're a lot more expensive than a regular bike."

"We've been saving up," Jonnie said. "We can buy one and share it."

They were impressed. The bike was strong and light, but smaller than a regular bicycle.

"We made ours out of other bikes," Marty said, "but they always break down. I like this one."

"It's made from aircraft aluminium. It's extra strong, very light and well balanced."

"How much is it?" Jonnie asked.

"One hundred and fifty-five dollars."

'Wow, that much," Marty exclaimed. "That's three times what an ordinary bike is worth."

"It has extra strong wheels and spokes. A special gear in the hub and an extra strong fork and chain. That's why it costs so much."

"It's a real beauty," Marty said, "but we could never afford that much. It took us a long time to save up fifty-five dollars."

"These bikes are for professionals, not for doing back yard tricks, that's why they cost so much."

"We can do anything a pro can do," Jonnie said. "We've been learning from videos."

"You've been watching BMX videos," the shopkeeper said. "I have one here from the bike company. It will knock your socks off. Come over here and look at it."

Marty and Jonnie were amazed. The riders were climbing over obstacles, jumping on walls and doing somersaults with their bikes."

"I want to do tricks like that," Jonnie said. "Now I know why the bike costs so much, a normal bike would never last long doing those tricks."

"Maybe we can weld some braces on to our bikes," Marty said.

"That would make them too heavy," Jonnie answered, "and they wouldn't be balanced."

"What are we going to do?" Marty asked. "I want to do tricks like that."

"I have a second hand one on the back," the shopkeeper said. "Come and look at it."

The bike looked new.

"It's an earlier model of the bike inside, but made of tungsten steel instead of aluminium. It weighs a few pounds more but it is strong and well balanced."

"We could learn on that," Marty said, "but I doubt if we can afford it because it has never been used.

"I bought a lot from another dealer. This won't sell because of the new one. I have two of them. You can have both of them for one hundred dollars."

"Is that one hundred each?" Marty asked

"No, for the two of them."

"That's a good deal. We can give you fifty-five now and ten dollars a week for the rest."

"You're good customers. I'll do it."

After making some adjustments—Jonny had to extend the seat as high as it would go and Marty put his as low as he could—the boys showed the shopkeeper the few tricks they could do. He was impressed and loaned them the video so they could learn more tricks. They spent every spare minute learning new tricks.

After a few weeks and some cuts and bruises, they were proud of what they could do.

A few weeks later, when the boys paid the shopkeeper the last payment, they gave him a demonstration of what they had learned.

"You're as good as the professionals," the shopkeeper said. "When you leave school you can join the circus."

CHAPTER THREE

Marty was often alone because Jonnie practiced with the basketball team and worked with his uncle occasionally.

Fred Quigley was a handyman. He could fix just about anything. He had a large shed full of all types of machinery and tools. Jonnie and Marty spent a lot of time there. That was where they tinkered with their bicycles.

Freddie, as he liked to be called, was Jonnie's uncle and foster father. He and Martha lost their only child when it was an infant and Jonnie and Marty took its place. Freddie taught the boys how to use the tools and even to weld.

Freddie had a medium sized truck he used to haul goods for a few clients. He also drove an armoured van for a small security company. Jonnie would help his uncle with deliveries after school, and on weekends and during school vacations.

This meant Marty had a lot of spare time. He would practice it the yard or watch videos on rainy days.

On the way to the video shop, Marty would ride past an abandoned building. He always wondered what was inside. One day, when he did not have anything to do, he rode down the lane behind the building. The back gate was broken so he looked around the rear yard. He soon found a way in and liked what he saw: a large empty room. On one side was a bench and a car lift.

This must have been a garage, he thought. *I'll clean it up so we can practice in here out of the weather.*

Marty removed the junk, swept the floor and repaired the rear door. He put a padlock on the door so no one else could get in, then he showed it to Jonnie.

"This is perfect," Jonnie exclaimed. "We have a clubhouse. What will happen to us if the owners find out?"

"No one has been near here for a long time," Marty said. "They will only toss us out, we haven't damaged anything.

'We can get a trampoline now," Jonnie said. "I always wanted a trampoline."

Jonnie had to tell Freddie about the clubhouse because they found a trampoline at a garage sale. It was too big for them to move.

"This is great," Freddie said. "I know the owner, he's a customer of mine. He wants to tear this down and build an apartment block here but he can't raise the money. He'll be glad to know someone is taking care of the building."

Freddie helped the boys by fixing the overhead door and the compressor.

They had their own workshop. Freddie kept his truck there and stored a few things he picked up. Everyone was happy.

One afternoon when it was raining the boys were practicing their tricks. They stopped for a break.

"You know," Jonnie said, "we've never been upstairs. Let's look around up there."

The stairs were at the back of the room near the rear door. They were steep and there were a lot of them because the ceiling was high. They came into a large open space all along the back of the building. Towards the front side were three doors.

The first one opened into an office that was above the overhead door and overlooked the road. Everything was still there: the desk, chairs and file cabinet.

"This is neat," Jonnie said. "We can start a business now."

"The only kind of business you know is, monkey business," Marty replied.

A door led into a large bathroom with a toilet stall. There was a door to the back room and another door that surprised the boys when they opened it.

The whole far side of the top floor was an apartment. Two bedrooms and a large lounge-kitchen combination. It was furnished, including a refrigerator.

"Wow," Jonnie exclaimed, "we can live here. This is great."

"Maybe later when we leave school. I don't want to leave my mother on her own right now."

They roamed around, looking in the closets. On the way-out Marty said, "We can put the mats up here and keep the downstairs open for our bikes."

"That's a good idea, it's getting crowded down there."

"What's that door underneath the stairs?" Marty asked.

Jonnie had trouble opening it because the hinges were rusted.

"There are stairs here," Jonnie exclaimed. "There's a cellar."

The cellar was a big empty cavern with a lot of columns holding up the upper floor. In the far corner was a long bench and some funny looking machinery.

"This is a large car hoist," Jonnie said. "What a silly place to put it. They can't get a car on it."

"Look up," Marty said. "The ceiling is wooden planks. The lift goes up through the ceiling."

"That's a weird place for a hoist," Jonnie said. "Wonder what they used it for?"

"They could store cars down here," Marty answered. I" bet it used to be an old repair pit then they put a lift in it."

"There are a bunch of old tools on the bench," Jonnie said. "You could be right. Come on, it's supper time."

***

The boys were happy. They had a clubhouse and money to buy all the equipment they wanted. They kept busy cleaning the back yard and around the front of the building. There were also learning trampoline tricks. They could bounce up and touch the ceiling. The trampoline and bicycle obstacle course were on the ground floor. Upstairs was the gymnastic equipment, including a tightrope strung close to the floor.

Marty spent more time at the clubhouse than Jonnie because Jonnie practiced basketball after school and helped his uncle on weekends and school holidays.

Jonnie rode in the armoured car a few times in the afternoons. Frankie gave him a hat and vest and told the customers that he was an apprentice.

One Friday afternoon during school vacation, Freddie stopped at the government bank.

"You can help me move the bags, there are quite a few of them."

On the way to the depot, Jonnie asked Freddie what was in the bags.

"They're full of money. Old worn out notes. They will be taken to the incinerator tomorrow morning and burnt."

"Can I go with you? I'd like to see that."

"We're paid extra for working Saturdays so we take turns. I'll take you when it is my turn."

"How often do they burn the money?"

"Once a month. All the banks send their money to the government bank and we take it away the last Friday in the month."

They drove into the depot and left the truck in the yard.

"I'm the last truck and I don't have to be emptied so it stays out overnight."

Frankie left the keys under the mat. He let Jonnie out the back gate then locked it and met Jonnie at the employee's entrance after he clocked off."

One afternoon after school Marty stayed to watch Jonnie practice. Marty was slightly jealous because Jonnie had friends on the team. Marty was self-conscious and shy so Jonnie was his only friend.

He didn't stay long. He remembered he had left his jacket in his locker so went to retrieve it. As he was leaving, he heard some sounds coming from the gym so he walked around the corner to see what was going on. To his surprise, he saw a girl going through a gymnastic routine. The thing that surprised him was the girl was as small as he was.

Marty was fascinated. He stood watching her different moves. She was good. Finally, she sprinted across the mat somersaulted, then leapt up and dove straight down toward the mat. Marty gasped, he thought she would injure herself, but she rolled her shoulder and somersaulted into a standing position. Marty was so excited he applauded.

The girl stiffened and looked annoyed so Marty said, "That was spectacular. I have never seen that routine before. Will you teach me how to do It?"

The girl walked to the rail and said, "I didn't know anyone was here. I'm practicing for the state championships in two weeks. It took me a year and lots of bruises to learn that. I doubt if you could do it."

Marty leapt over the rail and dove toward the floor. He rolled into a ball and flipped into a standing position.

"I can land that way but I like your way better. Will you teach me your move?"

"We're not supposed to practice without a supervisor in case we get hurt. The teachers won't stay after school so we can't use the gym."

"That's all right. I have my own gym. You can teach me there."

"No one has their own gym, the equipment is too expensive."

"I have everything here, and a trampoline too."

"You have a trampoline? I want to learn a trampoline routine but the school won't allow them because they're too dangerous. I priced them but they are too expensive for my parents to buy one for me."

"I got a big professional one at a garage sale. It has a covering over the springs. It's very safe."

"You are tempting me. Do you live close by? I have to be home when my parents come home at six."

"Three blocks from here on Orchard Street. You teach me your move and I'll teach you how to bounce."

The girl laughed then said, "It's a deal. I have seen you is some of my classes but you never speak to anyone. My name's Gloria Cloutier. What's yours?"

"I'm Marty McAlister. I don't have many friends because people laugh at me. That's why I don't talk to anyone at school."

"I'm the same size as you and I have lots of friends. I admit kids made fun of me but I got over it. My best friend is three times taller than I am. She's a basketball star."

"My only friend is three times taller than I am and he is also the star of the boy's team." They both laughed then Marty said, "We'd better go if you want to be home by six."

Marty had to ride very slowly because Gloria's bike was like his old one was, a one speed junior bike. Gloria was a bit hesitant about going into the old building.

"Come on," Marty said. "We keep it scrubby looking so no one will bother us."

Gloria was surprised when she saw the trampoline. She jumped on it right away. After bouncing for awhile they sat on the floor and Gloria said, "That was great. Will you really teach me how to properly use the trampoline?"

"Sure I will. I want to learn how to dive and recover like you do."

"How can we do that? There isn't any gum equipment here."

"We had to move it when we got the trampoline. It's upstairs. Come on, I'll show it to you."

"You're better equipped than the school," Gloria exclaimed. "You even have a proper tightrope."

"Jonnie and I practice here all the time, except when he's practicing basketball."

"It is the same with my friend, Sharon. She used to be very shy until she started playing basketball. The only time I see her now is at a game."

"You and I can be friends," Marty said, "and practice together."

"I like gymnastics," Gloria said, "but I'll never get anywhere with it."

"What are you saying? Of course you will. That routine I saw was perfect."

"I'm the best one on the team but I never win anything. Not even a place. The tall, skinny, long legged ones win all the time. Look at the time, I have to go."

On the way-out, Marty said, "Leave your bike here. I'll double you, then you'll get home sooner."

"I need the bike to go to school tomorrow."

"Leave it here. I have a better, faster one you can have."

They stopped at Marty's house and he gave her his old bike. He had to adjust the seat and dust it off.

"I had one like yours but I couldn't keep up to Jonnie so I made this one out of a couple bikes. It has a three-speed hub and two wheel brakes. You can have it because I have this one now."

As they rode along Gloria had a big smile on her face. "I'm scared, it goes so fast."

"We were wondering where you were," Gloria's mother said, as they arrived in the yard. "Who's your friend?"

"Mom and Dad, this is Marty, he's in my class. He has a trampoline and is going to teach me how to use it."

"Hello, Marty, why haven't we seen you before?"

"I'm very shy, most people laugh at me, so I keep to myself."

"Gloria had same problem but we helped her overcome it. Did your parents help you?"

"My mother is a teacher and understands children. I'm just very sensitive, that's all."

"That is a strange looking bicycle you have," Gloria's father said. "What kind is it?"

"It's a professional trick riding bike. It's very strong to handle the jumps."

"Can you do tricks with it?"

"Yes, sir, but there isn't any room here. I know, that's a strong picnic table. Sit at the far corner and I'll show you a couple of tricks."

Mr Cloutier sat at the far side edge of the table. Marty sat motionless on his bike then stood on the rear wheel, twisted, and climbed up onto the table, then down the other side. He came back beside the table, stood motionless, then jumped on to the seat, then on to the table. He moved backwards to the edge of the table then moved forward, stood on the rear wheel and turned around, then dropped on to the seat and then on to the ground.

They all applauded. "That was amazing," Mr Cloutier said.

"I was hesitant to allow Gloria to train on your trampoline, but now I know you're an expert so I won't object. We're pleased that Gloria has a new friend."

CHAPTER FOUR

It was the height of the basketball season, so Jonnie practiced every afternoon and worked with his uncle on Saturdays, so he did not spend much time with Marty or at the clubhouse. He was shocked one Friday afternoon when he arrived at the clubhouse and saw Marty and a girl going through a routine.

"What's she doing here? We agreed not to tell anyone about our clubhouse."

"Hi, Jonnie, I was going to tell you but I haven't seen very much of you lately. This is Gloria Cloutier, she's a gymnast. I'm helping her with her routine."

"Hi, Gloria, I've seen you at basketball practice"

"I'm a cheerleader for the girls' basketball team. We practice when the boys finish. My friend, Sharon Powers, is on the team. She'd like to meet you. She has seen you play and thinks you are the best."

"I have lots of fans but when they come close and see how tall I am they soon leave."

"You're not as tall as Sharon. She's the tallest girl in the school."

"Really, I will have to go to one of their games and watch her play."

"Great, there's a local game on tomorrow night. I'll introduce you. She will be thrilled. I have to go now. Nice meeting you, Jonnie, see you tomorrow night."

"Well, Marty has a girlfriend, I am impressed."

"She is not my girlfriend. We're just friends."

"Don't be silly, where else are you going to find a girl your size? She likes you and she's good looking. Time to grow up, Marty old pal."

Because it was a local game with another school there were not many people there. Gloria was sitting on the bench with the other girls. When she saw the boys come in, she ran to meet them.

"It's nearly game time. I didn't think you were coming. This is only a practice game so there aren't many supporters here. We'll talk at half time."

Jonnie was surprised and pleased when he saw Sharon. She was tall and slim with short brown hair and an intelligent face. He did not think much of her basketball skills. She moved up and down the court with the others but she was slow and hesitant. He thought she was only on the team because she was tall. She did not score many points.

Jonnie was very impressed when he met Sharon at half time. She was pleasant and easy to talk to.

After the game Gloria wanted to stop at a café to have a coffee and talk.

"Marty and I avoid public places," Jonnie said. "We don't like being laughed at."

"You are silly," Gloria replied. "The boys whistle at us but we ignore them."

"Girls can get away with that," Marty said, "but if we ignore a gang of boys they want to fight with us. I think they want to fight anyway."

"When we beat them up, we get blamed for starting it," Jonnie added."

"We'll go to my place," Sharon said. "I told my mother about you and she wants to meet you. She baked an apple pie for us."

The boys were surprised when they met Sharon's mother. She was nearly as tall as Sharon. Her father was average height. They had a nice conversation, getting to know each other.

The conversation turned to basketball. Sharon was bragging about how good Jonnie was. "He never misses the basket. I wish I was that good."

"I could teach you," Jonny replied, "but I don't have much spare time."

"We have time right now. Come out back and show me."

There was a concrete pad and a basketball hoop in front of the garage.

"I practice out here every day," Sharon said.

She picked up a ball, dribbled a few steps and tossed a basket. She tossed the ball to Jonnie, who was standing well back. He flipped it with one hand straight through the hoop.

"I can do that too," Sharon said. She walked up beside Jonnie, bounced the ball a few times and took careful aim. The ball bounced off the back rim. "I was close."

"The more you aim the harder it is to make the shot," Jonnie said. "You already know where the basket is, just toss the ball."

Sharon tried again but did the same thing. "I have a lot to learn, will you coach me?"

"I would love to, but I don't have any spare time. I hardly hang around with Marty any more."

"Come over tomorrow afternoon for a barbeque," Sharon's father said. "We go to church in the morning."

"I will if I can bring Marty along. We hardly see each other now."

"He's most welcome. You too, Gloria. We'll have a party."

***

The boys were up early. They rode to the skateboard ramp to practice. They did tricks on their bikes first then switched to skateboards. They were good. They could do all the tricks they had learned from videos. When some others arrived, they rode through the park.

The park had walls and stairs for them to practice on and picnic tables to climb over. Later they stopped at Marty's for a break, then they picked up Gloria and rode around until it was time for the barbeque.

Marty had been teaching Gloria some tricks. She could do a wheel stand and jump on to low walls. The first thing he taught her was how to balance on the bike while it was stationary. They had a good time riding through the park doing tricks.

When they arrived at Sharon's, they came down the drive doing a wheel stand then rode around the yard doing tricks.

"That was great," Sharon's father said. "You should put on shows, you're good."

"The public want more than a few simple tricks," Jonnie said. "Marty could handle breaking a few bones but mine would not heal properly. We just do easy tricks for our own entertainment."

They took their time over lunch then cleared away the table so they could play basketball.

"I played in high school and college," Sharon's father said. "I was pretty good." He sunk a few baskets then said, "Come on, Jonnie, one on one."

Jonnie smiled and stood near the basket. No matter how he tried, Sharon's father could not get past him and Jonnie would snatch the ball from him and pop it into the basket.

"You are good. I can easily get around Sharon."

"When I finish coaching her she should be as good as I am."

"I hope so," Sharon said. "Come on, let's get started." She picked up the basketball and said, "I want to sink baskets like you do."

Jonnie took the ball from her and rolled it into the corner. "All in good time. You have to learn the basics first. How fast can you run?"

Jonnie had Sharon run up and down the drive a few times. She could run a lot faster than he could. Then he gave her the basketball and told her to dribble it as fast as she could up and down the drive. She could not dribble very fast.

"Can you see what you are doing wrong? You practice in this confined space. That slows you down. Now get by me and sink a basket."

Sharon was no better than her father. She could not get around Jonnie and he could take the ball away from her anytime he pleased.

"I'll never be as good as you," Sharon moaned.

"Don't give up yet. You have just started. I am just showing you your faults. Next I will teach you how to overcome them."

The others watched for a while but it was going to be a long afternoon. The parents went in the house and Marty and Gloria went for a walk. The park was close by so they went there.

Gloria put her arm through his and said, "Marty do you like me?'

"Of course I do. Why would you ask me that?"

"I know we're friends. I want to know if you like me."

"What do you mean? Like boyfriend and girlfriend?"

"Yes, that's what I mean. Do you like me enough to be my boyfriend?"

"I don't know. You're the only girl I have ever hung around with. Until now it has only been Jonnie and me. Jonnie said I have to grow up and ask you to be my girlfriend. Do you want to be my girlfriend?'

"Of course I do, that's why I'm asking you if you like me."

"All right, what do I have to do? I've never had a girlfriend before."

"Well, we hang around together and you can walk to school with me."

"That will be hard because I ride to school with Jonnie and you ride with Sharon."

"You can meet me after school, they practice basketball."

"All right, we will do that. Is that all?"

They walked for a bit. Then Gloria said, "When a couple are going steady, they kiss. You can kiss me."

"I've never kissed anyone. I don't know what to do."

"I'll teach you. Put your arms around me." They stopped and Gloria turned toward Marty.

"What, right here. Now?"

"We're going steady, we can kiss any time we want. Now put your arms around me and pucker up your lips."

Marty loosely held Gloria and moved his face close to hers. She pulled him closer and pressed her lips to his. After a second Marty pulled back.

"That wasn't so bad," Gloria said. "Did you like it?'

"I guess so, I don't know."

"You need some practice. I'll have to teach you how to kiss properly."

She pulled Marty to her and held him tight so he could not get away. This time Marty could feel her lips and her body tightly against his. It was a warm, exciting sensation.

"I liked that, it made me feel good."

"You will feel good all the time after we practice some more."

Walking back Marty asked Gloria, "Can we practice kissing instead of doing your gymnastic routine?"

Gloria laughed and said, "Marty dear, we're going steady now, we can kiss any time and all the time from now on."

The others were sitting at the table eating pie and coffee.

"Come and join us," Sharon's father said. "We saved you some pie."

They talked for a while then Sharon said, "I want to show you what Jonnie has taught me. I'm not very good yet but I will get better as I practice."

Sharon stood in the drive and Jonnie stood near the basket. She charged down the drive dribbling as fast as she could, right at Jonnie. He tried to stop her but she turned sideways and pushed him closer to the basket. Then she sunk the ball.

Everyone cheered.

Sharon caught the ball and moved around Jonnie. He had a hard time trying to take the ball from her. Then they sunk a few baskets and quit for the day.

"That is enough for today," Sharon said. "I will practice all week and you can teach me something else next Sunday."

"We'll go for a ride to the beach," Sharon's father said. "I'll treat you all to a hamburger."

CHAPTER FIVE

Marty and Jonnie were on their way home one night during the week, after doing tricks in the park, when they heard shouting from a laneway as they passed by.

They stopped to look and saw three men beating up another man.

"We have to help that poor man," Jonnie said.

"They're tough guys, not schoolboys," Marty replied.

Before Marty could say anything else, Jonnie shouted, "Where are you mate? We're coming."

The men stopped, looked around then Jonnie made a lot of noise like there was a gang running. The men ran off down the lane.

"Thank you, boys," the man said. £You came just in time."

"You look pretty bad, we'll call an ambulance and get you to the hospital."

"No, please don't do that, I am well known and it will be in the papers. I do not want the publicity. Help me to my car. I'll be all right."

With one on each side, they walked the man about a block to his car. It was obvious that he was in a bad way and could not drive.

"We're going to take you to the hospital," Jonnie said. "You're in a bad way."

"No, please, take me home. I'll call a friend who is a nurse. He will take care of me."

Jonnie was not old enough to have a licence but he could drive. His uncle let him drive his truck on the back streets. They were soon at a large upper-class apartment building. The man directed them to his parking spot then they rode up the lift to his floor. They removed his shoes and outer clothes and sat him in a recliner. Marty found some aspirin in the medicine cabinet and Jonnie cleaned his wounds. They gave him a robe and made him comfortable.

"Can I get you anything?' Jonnie asked.

"I would love a cup of tea if it's not too much trouble."

Marty made the tea while Jonnie talked with the victim.

"What did you do to make those guys mad at you?" Jonnie asked.

"I am Martin St Clare, you have probably read about me in the papers. I am a well know lawyer and have just saved a big-time crook from a long jail sentence."

"Why would they beat you up if you saved their boss from going to jail?"

Martin laughed and said, "This is another gang. They have some compromising evidence against me and are blackmailing me. I refused to pay so they roughed me up a bit. The evidence would cause a small scandal but not enough to really hurt me so I refused to pay. They will try again. I will have to be careful."

"What if they give the evidence to the papers?"

"If they do that, they will not get any money. They want the money."

"Maybe we can help," Marty said, when he served the tea.

"Thank you, but what could you young fellows do?

"We could spy on them and maybe find something you could use against them."

"I appreciate you trying to help but these crooks are tough. You could be hurt if they found out you were spying on them."

"Don't worry about us. No one pays any attention to a boy on a skateboard," Marty said. "Tell us who they are and we will be careful."

"I really shouldn't do this but I'm desperate. The fellow is Martin McCauley. Be careful, you saw what they did to me."

"Don't worry, Mr St Clare, we will let you know what we find out. We have to go now, it's getting late and our parents will worry about us."

"Are you crazy?" Jonnie said, as they rode home. "These are tough crooks. It is too dangerous."

"The other crooks were tough too but we beat them," Marty answered. "Besides we need some more money if we want to keep up our new lifestyle. We have girlfriends now."

Jonnie tried to persuade Marty from spying on the crooks but Marty did not have anything else to do when he was not with Gloria, so he rode around looking for Mr McCauley.

That Saturday, Jonnie changed his mind and encouraged Marty to find the crooks. When he went to help his uncle, he was given a letter.

"It's from your landlord," Freddie said. "He's pleased that someone is taking care of his property."

Jonnie opened the letter and read it. "I don't understand. This is a rate notice from the council. It is for two hundred dollars."

"The landlord said he would not charge you any rent but expects you to pay the rates and electricity. He said he would give you a month's notice if he decides to tear it down. Also, he will give you first refusal if he decides to sell it. I think that is a fair proposition. He could get three hundred dollars a week for that place."

Jonnie read the notice again then said, "I suppose that is cheap rent for such a large building. Marty and I can afford two hundred dollars a year."

Freddie laughed and said, "Read the notice again. That is a quarterly bill. You have to pay two hundred dollars every three months plus fifty dollars for water and sewerage. You also have to pay your electricity bill every month."

Jonnie stared at his uncle. "We can't afford anything like that," he exclaimed. "I make twenty dollars a week working for you and Marty makes ten dollars a week cutting his mother's lawn. Besides, we have girlfriends now and they are expensive."

Freddie laughed again. "Welcome to the real world. It costs a lot to live in Sydney."

When Jonnie told Marty later that day his friend said, "What are you worried about? We have about a thousand dollars in the kitty to back us up."

"That's only a year's rent and there isn't much left to take the girls out."

"Relax, I found out where the crooks hang out. Mr St Clare will give us a reward when we find some evidence against them."

They spent the afternoon at Sharon's and went to the movies that night.

***

The girl's team was playing an important game that Thursday night. Marty and Jonnie were there. Sharon had slowly tried out her new skills at a couple of earlier games. The coach saw some improvement in her and encouraged her to take a more active part in the game. She sunk a couple of long baskets so the other team paid more attention to her. One of the aggressive girls pushed her a couple of times.

I'll fix her, Sharon thought. When she was passed the ball, instead of trying for a long shot, she charged down the court straight for the aggressive girl. Sharon turned sideways and bumped the girl. She ended up on the floor and Sharon sunk a basket, grabbed the ball and sunk another one. There was a roar from the crowd as Sharon returned to centre court with her hands in the air. The team had a new star player.

Jonnie and Marty were jumping and cheering and Gloria was doing cartwheels.

When Marty was not training with Gloria, he would be scouting around on his skateboard spying on Mr McCauley. His business was a block behind the shopping centre, a large two storied building with a laneway and a parking area. It was a brothel, the largest one outside of central Sydney.

Marty would skate around the block and occasionally through the parking lot, looking for a spot close enough to spy on the occupants. He was becoming desperate because he could not find a suitable location.

The building fronted the main street with a paved parking lot beside it. The parking lot ran to the laneway. There was a side door near the rear of the building, then a garage that opened on to the parking lot. After the garage was a tall fence that ran from the garage to the laneway, then along the laneway to the next building. There were no trees for Marty to hide in.

Marty would skate down the laneway then into the parking lot. He would skate around the parking lot doing tricks, looking around all the time. Then he would go around the block again.

One day, out of desperation, Marty stopped in the lane, turned his skateboard on its edge, stood on it and looked over the fence. Finally, he had found a hiding place to spy on the building.

Behind the garage there was a paved open space with an outdoor table and chair set and a potted tree. At the back of the building was a glass sliding door leading into a small office. There was a desk, a chair and a tall safe in the corner. Down along the fence were some large crates stored there. Marty realized he could hide behind the crates and observe the office. He returned home to plan his surveillance.

Marty and Jonnie were enjoying life. They were active, Jonnie with basketball and Marty with Gloria. They had friends and girlfriends plus a little money. Jonnie forgot about their expenses and enjoyed being the star of the basketball team. Marty was busy with Gloria and his surveillance of the gangsters. They did not have time to worry about what other people thought of them.

Sharon idolized Jonnie. He coached her into being the star of the girl's team and he was the star of the boy's team. They spent every moment they could with each other.

Jonnie practically lived at Sharon's. He had most of his evening meals there. His mother only saw him when he came home to go to bed. Marty had to go to Sharon's house on the weekends to see Jonnie.

Things stayed that way until the basketball season ended. Then Jonnie and Sharon would hang around the clubhouse with Gloria and Marty.

As with young people after they decided to go steady, Gloria and Marty's romance became serious. At first, they would kiss a lot when they met, to practice. Then, after the state gymnastic champions, where Gloria won the individual free style event, with her sensational dive; things became much more serious.

Gloria no longer had to practice so she and Marty spent more time kissing, which led to more intensive lovemaking. Soon they were spending a lot of time in one of the bedrooms. A couple of times Gloria told her parents that she was staying at Sharon's but spent the night with Marty.

When Sharon and Jonnie started hanging around the clubhouse, Marty and Gloria were becoming frustrated until Jonnie asked Marty if Gloria would mind if he and Sharon spent some time in one of the bedrooms. The clubhouse became a love nest.

Whenever Marty had some free time, he would ride his bike to the laneway. He had a hiding place near the brothel. He made a small ladder that he would hang on the fence to quickly climb over. He would hide behind the crates and spy on the office. He had a small but powerful telescope to see the dial on the safe. He planned to learn the combination and sneak in when the office was empty and clean out the safe.

The only flaw in his plan was the gangster only opened the rear door when he was there and only on a warm afternoon.

Marty soon learned the gangster's habits. He was there for about an hour late in the afternoon. When he left he locked the doors. Marty was ready to quit when he got his break.

The gangster was sitting at his desk with the safe open and some papers spread out on the desk. Nothing happened and Marty was thinking of going home when a man came into the office and told the boss he had an important phone call.

Instead of putting everything away, he got up and left the room, locking the inside door. Marty did not hesitate. He jumped up, dashed across the porch and into the office. He had a cloth paperboy's bag which he quickly filled up with everything he could grab in the safe. Then he picked up all the papers on the desk and the ones from an open briefcase. He tossed the briefcase into the safe and shut the door and spun the dial. Then he dashed out and over the fence and did not stop until he was nearly home. He kept looking behind him on the way. He went to the clubhouse and collapsed on the trampoline. He was still there when Jonnie came looking for him.

"Are you all right? Your mother called me, you didn't come home for supper. What happened to you?"

"I broke into the gangster's office and stole everything in his safe. I am never going to do that again. I was so scared I nearly fainted right there in his office."

"Marty, you are crazy. What if you had been caught? You would have disappeared. We would never see you again."

"I didn't get caught and no one knows I did it. We're rich. There was a lot of money in the safe. I took all of it."

"We will hide the bag in the basement and look at it later. I have to get you home, your mother is worried about you."

"I exercised too hard, Mom, and fell asleep," Marty told his mother.

"I found him asleep on the trampoline," Jonnie added.

"I waited a half an hour for you," Marty's mother said. "I was worried so I called Jonnie. I am glad it was nothing serious. Why do you have to practice so much?'

"We usually take turns but Jonnie was not there so I kept on going, that's all."

"Next time don't wear yourself out. You could be hurt with no one there to help you."

Marty was exhausted. He ate his supper and went to bed. He didn't see Jonnie until early Saturday morning.

"We only have an hour before we pick up the girls," Jonnie said. "I'm curious to see what you got."

They went into the basement and dumped the contents of the bag on the bench. There were a lot of papers, envelopes and a pile of money.

"Look at all this stuff," Jonnie exclaimed. "It will take a long time to go through all of this."

"We'll separate it and take what we think is important to Mr St Clare," Marty said. "We will keep the rest until we find out what it is."

"There are a couple of journals in here too," Jonnie said. "I bet Mr St Clare will be very interested in them. We will have to visit him soon."

"We can't see him until Monday night," Marty said. "We have dates with the girls tonight and tomorrow. Put it away for now."

CHAPTER SIX

Around noon on Monday the police were called to the brothel. There was a disturbance there and shots were fired. The street was blocked off and the rapid response squad was called. By late in the afternoon order was restored but the brothel was closed with a police guard.

When the big boss came on Monday morning to collect the weekend takings, he was told by the gangster that the safe had been robbed. The boss called his boys and the gangster barricaded himself in the building. There were a lot of very nervous, important people hoping that there was nothing found in the records that would say they had visited the establishment.

Marty and Jonnie made excuses to the girls and went straight to the clubhouse. The first thing they did was count the money. Five thousand two hundred fifty dollars.

"We are rich, Jonnie exclaimed. "We can buy this building now."

"We will continue on the same as we have been. We do not want anyone asking questions, Marty replied.

They separated the papers. They found a stack of A4 envelopes with names on them. Mr St Clare's name was among them. Inside was a couple of photographs of Mr St Clare with a naked woman.

"Looks like Mr St Clare visited the brothel," Jonnie said. "They thought they could cash in on it."

"I would think that would give the place a bad name," Marty replied.

"Who's going to tell? No one would admit to going there."

Jonnie called Mr St Clare from a pay phone to tell him to expect them that evening.

After supper, Marty and Jonnie rode to the apartment block, slid under the parking barrier and rode the lift up from the basement. Mr St Clare was surprised when they knocked on his door.

"How did you get in here? This place is secure. We pay extra for that."

"You're wasting your money," Jonnie said. "If a couple of kids can get in here, what could real crooks do?"

"Mr St Clare, you asked us to get something on the gangster. "Well, we did," Marty said. "Here are the photos they had of you."

"Wonderful. How did you get them? I doubt if they will bother me again anyway. Have you seen the news tonight?"

"No sir," Jonnie answered, "we were on our way over here. What has happened?"

"It will be on the seven o'clock news. Have a look."

They watched as the news presenter said, "The centre of Alexandria was under siege this afternoon when two rival gangs fought over possession of the notorious Nightingale brothel. It took the riot squad three hours to subdue the fighters and restore order. Three well known criminals were arrested along with six others, two of whom required hospital treatment. The mayor complained that he has been after the police to close the place ever since he has been mayor."

"Wow," Jonnie said, "we must have shaken the hornets' nest."

"All I did was to take a few things out of the safe," Marty exclaimed.

"I don't believe it," Mr St Clare exclaimed. "You caused all this?"

"Yes, sir I was spying on the gangster, trying to get something you could use, when he left his office, so I dashed in, grabbed a few things and dashed out again. That's all."

"That's all. Son, you have done me and a lot of others a great service. I am in your debt. Is there anything I can do for you?"

"I can't think of anything right now. Later we want to start a business and buy a property. Maybe you can help us with that."

"Son, I will be your legal representative for life. That is the least I can do. I thought you would ask me to put you through college. We will celebrate, I have some cola in the fridge."

Mr St Clare was very happy. He had the incriminating evidence against himself and the gangster was in jail.

"I never thought I would see you boys again," he said. "You are remarkable and very brave to do such a thing."

"I was so scared," Marty said, "I almost fainted right there in his office."

They laughed, then Jonnie handed Mr St Clare the journals. "Marty found these too."

Mr St Clare looked through them then said, "These are dynamite. This one is the financial record of the brothel. The tax people will have a ball with that. The other one is a record of the money he has been blackmailing from other influential people. It seems I was not the only one involved. The last entry is from the mayor for five hundred dollars. The total is five thousand two hundred and fifty dollars. They have a good thing going."

Marty and Jonnie smiled.

"If there is anything I can do for you boys just let me know," Mr St Clare said. "You have made me very happy today."

"There is one small thing," Jonnie said.

"I will do anything I can to help you. Come and see me when you decide to start your business. By the way, what are you planning to do?"

"Well, neither of us could hold down a normal job," Marty said, "so we were thinking of someday going into business for ourselves but we don't know what is a good business to get into."

"The good ones are real estate or the stock market. Spend your last year in school learning about them, then take a business course at tech. That will give you a solid foundation for your business. Along the way, you may find something else you would like to do."

"Thank you, Mr St Clare," Marty, said, "that is good advice. We have to go now, it's getting late."

"Thank you again, boys, and drop by anytime I like talking to you. By the way, Jonnie, what is that small favour you were going to ask me?"

"I forgot, you know that journal with all the names in it? Well, we have their files too. Just like yours. What shall we do with them?"

Mr St Clare had to sit down. He could not speak for a minute. Finally he said, "You boys are unbelievable. You can make a fortune selling them back to the victims."

"Would you have paid us for your file?"

"I understand what you mean. I would have but I would have hated you and tried to get back at you."

"We don't want all those people hating us," Jonnie said.

"All right, I know most of them. Some of them are friends of mine. I will find a way to return them or let them know they have been destroyed. Leave it with me. Come back in a few days, I will have a plan by then. Good night, boys."

The boys spent the next few days with the girls. It was near the end of the school year. There were exams to study for and there was the end of the year dance to prepare for. Jonnie and Sharon were voted as prince and princess. Marty and Gloria were going too.

The boys had some time to themselves while the girls were studying so they went through the rest of the articles from the safe.

"This guy liked to write," Marty said. "He has a diary on himself and his cronies. Here is a diary on some other gangsters. I bet the police would love this."

"You walk into the station and hand it to them," Jonnie said. "They will arrest you for burglary."

"We would be doing a service to the community," Marty replied.

'I know," Jonnie said, "there's a detective who stops at the coffee shop in the square every morning. We could ride by and drop it into his car. He rides around with the window open."

"How do you know that?"

"My mother stops there too, she talks with him. I think she likes him."

"All right, we'll do it," Marty said, "but we have to make sure we wipe every page clean so it can't be traced back to us."

Jonnie stopped at the coffee shop to ask his mother for a dollar. She was sitting with the detective. She introduced him to her friend.

Marty skated past the car and tossed the envelope through the open window.

"That was slick," Marty said, when they met up later.

"The policeman seems like a nice man," Jonnie said. "He told me to join the Police Youth Club. They have a basketball team."

"You're not going to do that, are you?"

"We could stop by and have a look. Maybe teach them a trick or two."

CHAPTER SEVEN

Ida Eastwood was a fair looking lady in her mid-thirties. She had let herself go when she separated from her husband and moved to Sydney, but then started to rebuild her self-esteem when she found a good job. Jonnie was no trouble other than he kept to himself. She was glad when he met Marty.

With spare time and nothing to do, Ida started her rejuvenation by going to the hairdresser. Then she bought some new clothes. Occasionally she would go shopping with her brother's wife, Martha. But Martha was a housewife so Ida went to the art gallery and local concerts for something to do. Her favourite indulgence was the coffee shop near where she worked. After bumping into Francis Banks, the tough detective, a couple of times, they would sit together and talk over their coffee.

Francis used to grab a take away coffee and drink it on the run. Now he sat and talked to Ida.

When Jonnie came in, that broke the ice and after he left Ida said, "Now that you have met my son, I can invite you to supper one night."

"I would love that, but don't be disappointed if I don't show up. I never know what the day will bring.

That is why I am single and lonely. I have disappointed too many people too many times."

"I will put the supper in the oven and keep it warm for you."

Francis did not notice the envelope on the passenger seat until later that day. He had made other stops so he did not know where it came from. It caused a sensation in his department when he emptied it on his desk.

After a long discussion with the superiors, it was decided that the evidence was not valid unless the author would testify in court that he wrote it.

"Any one of you could have written that," the chief said. "We have to get Mr McCauley to admit he did it."

"He will never do that," Francis said. "He would not last a day on the street after he testified."

"We have him for firearms offences and we can add attempted murder to that," the chief said. "He will get at least five years for that. We will give him a new identity. He may go for it, after all he still has to contend with his boss, who is blaming him for the theft."

"We know he did not steal anything," Francis said. "The one who tossed this into the car was the thief."

A couple of nights later, when Jonnie came in from skateboarding, he was surprised to find Detective Banks sitting at the kitchen table drinking wine with his mother.

"There you are, Jonnie," his mother said. "I invited Francis over for supper. Jonnie rides his skateboard at night when there is no one at the ramp."

"There are no lights there," Francis said. "You could hurt yourself."

"I've been doing it for years. Marty and I go at night so no one will taunt us. We don't like getting into fights."

Jonnie said, "Goodnight," and went to his room.

"He's a strange boy," Francis said.

"His father used to call him a freak. It hurt him badly. He has improved a lot since he has been on the basketball team. He has a girlfriend on the girls' basketball team. They look like twins."

"I have seen him play, he is very good."

Francis soon became a regular visitor at the McAlister's home.

Marty and Jonnie were keen to get rid of the blackmail files so they wiped every one of them with a clean cloth and packed them in plastic bags.

"These are well known important people," Marty said. "You would think that they would know better than visit a brothel."

"Life must be tough at home," Jonnie added.

"Are we going to do the same when we are older?" Marty asked. "I don't think I want to be an adult. They either spend their time at the pub or in a brothel. I don't understand it. My parents do not do that and neither do Sharon's"

"My father argued with my mother all the time," Jonnie said. "I don't know why. I was too young and I would never ask my mother. I know she wants to forget all that. I remember my mother cried a lot. You are right thinking about being an adult is scary."

Mr St Clare was pleased to see them. "I thought you had forgotten me. You will be pleased with the arrangements I have made. We both are going to profit from this."

"What do you mean by profiting?" Jonnie asked. "We are not going to blackmail anyone."

"Let me explain. Some of these people are good friends of mine so I invited them to a poker night. I told them I had hired one of my former clients, who had a grudge against Mr McCauley, to retrieve my incriminating evidence. When I told them he had taken all the files, they all agreed to share the expense."

"You are charging these people for the return of their files?" Marty asked.

"No, no. They volunteered to contribute a little to help me defray the costs involved. That's all."

"I still don't understand," Jonnie said. "They are going to pay you for the return of their files?"

"They are relieved to know the police did not find the files and are happy to pay to get them back. It is a lot less than Mr McCauley was charging them."

"Just explain it to us in plain English," Jonnie said.

"All right, after explaining the danger that my man faced in retrieving the documents, they all agreed to contribute one hundred dollars each in appreciation for what he had done. They agreed on the amount, not me. Granted, they had no idea how many files there were and I did not tell them. I explained the situation to the others. They have agreed that it is a fair settlement. Boys, we are rich. Fifty files at one hundred dollars each equals five thousand dollars."

Marty and Jonny were quiet absorbing what they had just been told. Finally, Mr St Clare said, "I think it is fair that we split the money in half. I will set up a company with a trust fund for you. When you are ready you can start a business."

"I am sure that is fair, Marty said, "and you know all about those things. We are going to do what you told us and study business for the last year of school. By then we should know what we want to do and we will have some money to get us started."

"You are very sensible, Marty. I will be here to help and advise you."

"We have a building we want to buy," Jonnie added. "Do we have enough money to buy it?"

Jonnie had to tell Mr St Clare all about their clubhouse. His advice was, "I know that building, it use to be a taxi depot. It is in a poor location and badly run down. That is why the owner cannot raise the funds to build apartments there. It is zoned for light industry. You have a good arrangement so leave things as they are. Sometime later you will decide what you want to do and if you waste your money on that old place you will not have anything to start your business with. That place will never sell."

"You are right, Mr St Clare I am glad you are advising us," Marty said. "We will ask for your advice before we do anything. Now we have to go. We will stop by again soon."

***

They always met at Sharon's on Sunday afternoon. Usually Jonnie and Sharon would practice basketball. Now the season was over, all they did was hang around.

"I think we should practice dancing for the ball on Friday night," Sharon said.

"We don't have to practice," Jonnie said. "Anyone can dance."

"Have you ever danced?"

"No, but we can move around without stepping on each other's toes."

"We are the prince and princess. We have to lead the grand waltz. Can you waltz?"

"Okay, you win. What do I have to do?"

"I will get Mother, she will teach us."

The others enjoyed watching Jonnie try to dance. He told them to leave because he could not concentrate while they were laughing.

Gloria was a good dancer. Part of here acrobatic routine was dancing. She taught Marty so they could do a routine together.

Gloria and Marty spent most of their time together with each other. Sharon and Jonnie were always practicing basketball. They enjoyed each other's company. They rode around for a while then sat on a bench in the park.

"Marty, I have something to tell you. My parents and I are going to Tasmania for Christmas. We are leaving the week after school closes and will not be back until the end of January."

"How come you're going for such a long time?"

"Mother and father both come from Tasmania so we are going to visit both families."

"Jonnie will be working with his uncle, so I'll be alone all that time."

"I'm sorry, Marty. You will find enough to do. The time will pass quickly."

"I like you, Gloria and have become use to you being around. I know I will be lonely."

"Please, Marty, I will be lonely too. I will send you post cards."

"You'll be back here before the postcards arrive."

Gloria laughed then said, "We can read them together and I can tell you all about the places I visited."

"This will be a good test for when we graduate and you go to college. We will be apart for a long time then."

"Let's not think about that now. We still have a year before we go to college."

"I'm not going to college. Jonnie and I are going to tech to study business procedures then start our own business instead. We have decided that we could not get a regular job so we are going to start our own business and work for ourselves."

"That's a great idea. Have you decided what kind of business you are going into?"

"No, we're going to study different ones for now then decide when we leave school. I like real estate and Jonnie is keen on the stock market. Maybe we can do both."

"You need a lot of money to start those businesses. You will have to work for someone else until you save up enough to start up on your own."

"We're going to put all the money we make away to help us get started."

"I will go to business college so I can be part of the company too."

"That would be great, Gloria. We have something to plan for now."

When Marty and Gloria returned, Jonnie and Sharon and her parents were waltzing around the back yard. Gloria and Marty joined them.

Jonnie could not rent a tuxedo. They did not have one that would fit him. Every afternoon he and his mother would visit men's clothing stores. Ida would usually buy long legged pants, extend the legs and take in the waist. Shirts were the hardest, Jennie's arms were longer than most shirts. Ida would cut the cuffs off and sew on an extension but this was a special occasion. Jonnie needed a tuxedo.

Finally, they found a theatrical hire shop that hired out clown costumes. They had a long-legged tuxedo. With a few alterations it fitted perfectly.

Jonnie looked older and more mature. He liked what he saw, but did not think much of having to wear a clown's costume.

Jonnie and Sharon were the celebrities of the ball. They were the prince and princess, the heroes of the basketball team, and they both looked stunning dressed up for the occasion. Sharon looked like Cinderella and Jonnie looked like a movie star. The audience loudly applauded as they led the grand waltz. They would remember the night for many years.

CHAPTER EIGHT

One afternoon a couple of weeks after the ball, Marty and Jonnie found a letter in a crack in the rear gate of the clubhouse. It was from Mr St Clare, the lawyer. He wanted to see them. They visited him that evening.

"I thought you boys had forgotten me. I have the papers for your company and a little favour to ask. We will have a cold drink and talk about it."

They sat in the lounge drinking lemonade. The boys told Mr St Clare about the summer prom. Then Mr St Clare explained their company to them.

"You are now the principals of a proud Australian company called Green and Gold Enterprises. I wanted an Australian name and was surprised that such a great Australian name was available. It cost one hundred dollars to search and register the company and you have to pay fifty dollars a year to keep the name. I will take care of that for you. Gentlemen, you are now registered businessmen, congratulations."

"I like real estate," Marty said, "and Jonnie is interested in the stock market."

"We are going to change to the business course next year," Jonnie said. "We will learn all we can about these businesses."

"You are on the right track," Mr St Clare said, "but keep an open mind. You may decide later on to do something entirely different. Now, I have a favour to ask you. This time there is no danger involved. A friend of mine is not getting along with her husband and wants to divorce him. The only way she can do that is to show that he has been unfaithful. That will be easy because he has a lady friend he has been seeing for at least a year. I want you to get some proof that he is unfaithful."

"How are we going to do that?" asked Jonnie.

"I have a special camera that uses high speed film that does not need a flash bulb. I want you to take some pictures of him with his girlfriend. Can you do that for me?"

"Now that school is out Marty has a lot of spare time," Jonnie said. "He can easily do it."

""Good, here are all the particulars, including his photograph. They mainly meet at lunch time at the girlfriend's flat."

""How did you get all this information?" Marty asked.

"His wife gave it to me. She has known about the affair for months."

"That should be enough for a divorce," Marty said. "Why do you need photographs?"

"She wants her half and alimony. She will get something if she divorces him, but he can claim she is divorcing him and will not have to pay her very much. The law is very messy on divorce."

"All right," Marty said, "I have plenty of time. I will get your pictures."

"Thank you, Marty, I knew I could count on you."

***

Freddie had a contract with a small soft drink company. It was easy during the cold months but nearly full time in the summer. Jonnie was helping him every day. Sometimes they would take Marty along. He would stay on the truck and pass the wooden cases to them and restack the empties. Otherwise, Marty spent a lot of time alone in the clubhouse.

One Friday afternoon Freddie took Jonnie with him in the armoured truck. They went to the bank to pick up fifteen money bags. The bags were large, something like mail bags, but they were bright blue and locked.

"It's my turn tomorrow to go to the incinerator," Freddie said. "Would you like to help me?"

"I have never been to the incinerator; it will be a new experience."

Jonnie waited at the gate. When it opened, he got in the truck with his uncle.

The incinerator was out on the bay so the smoke would blow out to sea.

"The government is going to close it down soon," Freddie said. "Too many people are complaining when the wind is blowing the wrong way, so this will be my last trip. I will not be driving this truck for much longer either. The company has been bought by a large security company. I don't meet their standards so I will retire when the company is sold."

"What will you do, Uncle? You need this job."

"I used to but now I have more work as a courier than I can handle so I will not miss this job. I will be getting a big redundancy pay out so I'm not worried."

The incinerator was a huge block of concrete. There was a long, wide ramp leading up to a large open bay. They drove in and backed up to a large bin. When they came in the barriers came down and the ramp was closed. They had to wait until the other trucks left before they could unload.

It was a complicated, slow process. The manager and his assistant came out. Marty handed Freddie the bags one at the time and Freddie put the bag down in front of the hopper. The manager had the key to unlock the bag. He opened it then reached in and handed a paper that was inside to his assistant. The assistant checked the number on the bag against the number on the paper, then the manager reached in the bag again and removed a red plastic bag. The bag was sealed. There was a large tag on it which the manager removed and handed to his assistant. He checked the tag against the number on the outer bag and the piece of paper. When all that was done, the manager told Freddie to toss the bag in the bin. Then the process would start all over again, fifteen times in all.

Finally, when the last bag was in the bin, the manager signalled to a man behind a window. There was a loud whirring noise, then the bin lifted up and an iron gate opened. Jonnie could see a deep red glow behind the open gate and feel the heat coming out. The bin tipped and the bags slid into the opening and the gate closed.

The manager, his assistant and Freddie went into the office to sign some papers. Jonnie gathered the empty bags and put them in the truck then Freddie came out and they drove off.

"That was really something," Jonnie said. "They make sure no one can get the money."

"What good would it do them? The notes are worn out."

Jonnie was thinking that you could spend an old note as easily as you could a new one. A plan was forming in his mind.

"Uncle, how long before you retire from this job?"

"About six weeks. My last official job will be picking up the old notes from the bank. They are going to retire about half the staff and most of the trucks. The bakery is going to buy some of them. They have the same kind of trucks in their fleet."

Jonnie paid careful attention when his uncle drove into the yard. He took his time and looked all around the yard. Uncle's truck was always the last one in and he hardly ever handled incoming money, so his truck stayed outside overnight. Freddie put the ignition keys under the mat then let Jonnie out the gate. Jonnie watched carefully when Freddie turned off the alarm so he could get out of the gate. He was smiling all the way home. He had the whole plan figured out before he got out of the truck. "I wonder what Marty is going to say when I tell him we are going to steal an armoured truck?" he thought as he went into the house.

***

Marty soon identified the adulterous husband. He followed him a few times to establish a pattern. No one noticed a boy on a skateboard. The fellow was very predictable. He had a set routine. Marty picked out a spot to photograph him and his girlfriend without being seen. He got some good shots of them walking arm in arm. All he needed were some bedroom shots. He needed Jonnie to help him with that.

Marty soon found the girlfriend's flat but could not reach the fire escape ladder. He needed Jonnie to toss him up so he could grab the last rung. He had Jonnie meet him one day at noon when they were delivering nearby.

Jonnie flipped Marty up to the ladder. Marty was so light that the ladder did not come down when he grabbed it. Jonnie hung around until Marty finished. It did not take long. Marty got some good shots. He crouched beside the window and peeked in. When he saw a good shot of the man's face he would take a quick picture. He did not stay on the fire escape for too long in case someone saw him.

"We'll take the film to Mr St Clare tonight," Jonnie said. "I want to keep the camera for a while. I have something I need to photograph. Buy a regular colour film for me."

Jonnie had not told Marty his grand plan yet. He was making sure that he had figured everything out so Marty could not object.

Marty walked with Jonnie to the shop where the drinks were being delivered. Freddie told Jonnie he was finished for the day so Marty and Jonnie walked home.

On the way Jonnie stopped to buy a colour film.

"Are you going to take some photos of me?" Marty asked.

"No, I have thought up a plan to make us rich, but I need some photos first. I will tell you about it when we get to the clubhouse.

"You are mad!" Marty exclaimed. "Steal an armoured truck, that is crazy."

"I have thought it all out. The timing is perfect. We will not get caught and we will be filthy rich."

Jonnie drew a diagram of the yard and gate. He explained the alarm and how to open the gate. Marty studied the plan then said, "You have figured it out except, how do I get in there? Will I have to sneak in when the gate is open and hide?"

"I hadn't thought of that. We'll ride around there and look for a way in. There may not be any place to hide in the yard. I did not think to look for one."

"It is a good plan," Marty said, "and with the confusion of the move we could get away with it."

"I knew you would like it. We have a lot to do, we only have six weeks. I need the camera to photograph a bakery truck. We have to make some signs to put over the security ones. To disguise the truck."

"You have thought of everything. We'll do it. Come on, we can ride around the bakery parking lot, it's always open."

Gloria and her family were in Tasmania, so Marty was alone. Jonnie was not doing any better. Sharon had a summer job working on her uncle's avocado farm on the North Coast. She would be away for most of the summer, so the boys had plenty of spare time to plan their heist.

Jonnie had taken an art course in school and one of the projects was making a montage with sticky back paper. He knew where to get some large sheets of this paper. They were going to draw the bakery logo on the paper then stick it over the security signs. They soon found out it was a lot harder than they thought.

"Let's stick a blank sheet on the sides," Marty said, "and only make small signs for the doors and back. It is going to be in the middle of the night so no one will notice."

"That's a great idea and we will save a lot of time."

"You have forgotten one thing," Marty said. "Where are we going to hide the truck?'

"We will hide it here, where else?"

"Your uncle and the girls will see it. We might as well leave it in the street."

"That's not a good idea, they might be able to trace it back to us. We will have to think of something or forget the whole idea."

"We have to think of something," Marty said. "I am dreaming of all that money already. The truck has to vanish completely. It must never be found."

"The only way we can do that is to drive it off the pier," Jonnie said. "Someone is bound to see us or find it right away."

"We have ninety-nine percent of a perfect plan," Marty said. "We have to think of a way to hide the truck."

They walked in circles around the gym trying to think of something. After a bit Marty said, "Never mind the truck, where are we going to hide the money?"

"That's easy," Jonnie said, "we will stash it downstairs, no one ever goes down there."

"Downstairs, that's it!" Marty shouted. "We hide the truck downstairs. It's perfect."

"What are you raving about? How are we going to get the truck down there?'

"The hoist, dummy, we drop it down the hoist then replace the floor, simple."

They whooped and hollered and ran around the room. When they calmed down, they went down to look at the hoist.

"What if it doesn't work?" Jonnie said. "We can't get anyone to fix it for us."

"I watched your uncle fix the one upstairs. He cleaned it up and put some oil in the compressor. We can do that."

The boys were busy preparing for the big heist. The hoist was in the far corner of the room. Large hardwood planks covered the opening. They had not been moved for many years. The planks were dirty and stained with oil. They looked like the surrounding floor. Jonnie and Marty struggled to loosen and remove them.

"It's going to be close," Marty said.

"What do you mean? That is a big hole."

"Maybe so, but so is the truck. What if it doesn't fit?"

"Nothing is going to stop us now," Jonnie exclaimed. "If it is to big we will chop it up and toss it down there."

After spending a lot of time cleaning and oiling the compressor they were ready to turn it on.

They had cleaned it. Topped up the crank case on the compressor with oil. Checked the belts and hoses.

Marty turned the compressor over by hand then said to Jonnie, "We have done all we can. Hit the switch."

There was a switch box on the wall next to the controls for the hoist. Jonnie opened the door and looked at the fuses inside then said, "Here goes," and threw the switch. Nothing happened.

They stood looking then Jonnie did it again. Nothing."

"I bet they removed the main fuses," Marty said. "Where is the fuse box?"

"It would be outside on the side of the building so the meter man can read the meter."

They ran around to the side of the building and lifted the cover of the meter box.

"Look at all the fuses," Marty said. "It will take all day to check them all."

"They are labelled," Jonnie said. "Upstairs, ground floor, basement. The basement area is here and here is the fuse that is labelled motor." Jonnie pulled out the fuse and examined it. "Nothing wrong with this, and the main switch is on. The motor must be burnt out."

They slowly walked back inside and sat down.

"What are we going to do now? Jonnie asked. We can't get anyone in here to look at the motor."

"Maybe the wire has been cut," Marty said.

"No one has been here for years," Jonnie said. "How would the wire have been cut?"

"Do you have any other ideas? Let's check the wire from the motor to the main fuse box. We have to try everything."

They had to do something so they went down to the compressor and carefully examined the wire from the motor to the switch.

"The wire is inside a cover," Jonnie said. "No one could cut it. Then it is in a metal pipe from here to the fuse box. The motor must be burnt out. We will have to buy a new motor."

"Don't give up yet," Marty said. "There has to be a reason why it doesn't work."

Marty followed the conduit along the wall to where it went outside to the fuse box. Suddenly he shouted, "Hooray! I found it."

Jonnie ran over and Marty pointed to an isolation box high on the wall. Jonnie opened the box and two fuses were laying inside. Jonnie quickly replaced them then they ran back to the control box. Jonnie threw the switch. The motor turned over and the compressor loudly started working. The boys were jumping around screaming and hugging each other.

"We're rich!" they were screaming over the noise of the compressor.

When they calmed down, they tried the hoist. It worked. Jonnie rode it up and down a couple of times. They put everything back in place and went home happy.

CHAPTER NINE

Everything was ready. They had to wait for the big day. The girls were away and Jonnie was working with his uncle so Marty was just hanging around. He would work with Jonnie for something to do. He was pleased when he found a letter from Mr St Clare their lawyer friend. They visited him that night.

"I have another favour to ask. It is rather dangerous so I will not mind if you refuse. A wife of one of my clients came to me. She wants to know if her husband is seeing another woman."

"I'm just hanging around," Marty said. "I can easily take a few photos for you."

"It's not that easy. This man is a well-known gangster. He is known for eliminating those he does not like. I have saved him from a long jail sentence more than once."

"If he is such a bad person ,why are you saving him from jail?" Jonnie said. "He deserves to be in jail."

"He has only been accused of disposing of other criminals. He is doing society a favour. Besides, I do very well defending him."

"I will do it as long as I only have to follow him and take some pictures," Marty said. "I will not get in a situation where I might be caught."

"All right, all my client wants is proof that he is seeing someone. She does not want to divorce him. Just confront him with the evidence."

Mr St Clare gave Marty a file with all the information he needed.

"I've seen his photograph in the paper," Marty said. "He's famous."

"He has a night club at the Cross," Mr St Clare said, "a couple of brothels and other businesses. He hangs out at the Italian coffee shop just off the mall. You will find him there almost every morning. Now, tell me what you have been doing during the school break."

"Jonnie has a job with his uncle," Marty said. "I help him sometimes otherwise I am just hanging around. Spying on this guy will give me something to do."

"Remember, he's dangerous. Do not take any chances. Also there are always a couple of his men close by. Be on the lookout for them."

On their way home Jonnie spoke to Marty. "Are you sure you want to do this? It sounds dangerous. What if you are caught? I need you to help me with the armoured car."

"What are they going to do to a kid? I'll tell them I'm trying to get a good shot for the newspaper. They will boot me in the bum and send me on my way."

"I suppose you are right, but this is the last time. We are about to become millionaires, so we shouldn't take any more chances. I am not going to try any new tricks in case I get badly hurt. You should do the same."

"I had not thought of that," Marty said. "We have a new exciting life ahead of us. You're right, we can't take any more chances. I wish you had thought of that before we saw Mr St Clare, I would have refused the job."

"This is only a few photos," Jonnie said. "He will not end up like the other fellow did."

"You don't know for sure if the badly burnt body they found in the National Park was him.

"Detective Banks told my mother he moved out of state," Jonnie replied.

"If it wasn't him it was his partner. Neither of them have been seen since we took the money."

"Maybe this guy's wife will shoot him," Marty said, "then there will be one less crook in town."

"He will just be replaced by another one."

Marty was busy for the next couple of weeks. It took him a couple of days to find his quarry. Then another few days to adjust to his routine. He was very predictable. Marty soon spotted his bodyguards and easily avoided them.

He followed the man around for a couple of weeks. Marty always wore different clothes. Sometimes he would be on his skateboard and other times on his bike.

Finally, he was sure that the man was not cheating. All he could get were shots of him with other men.

Marty was ready to give up the project. He decided that today would be the last time. He arrived at the coffee shop early to get a good shot. The fellow always sat in the courtyard at the same table. Marty would come in the back way and hide behind a lattice screen. He would put the camera up to a hole in the lattice for a good shot.

Marty was crouched in his favourite spot waiting for the fellow to arrive when two of his henchmen came in first and moved the tables around. They set them up right next to the lattice where Marty was hiding. Soon, six men came in a couple at a time and sat at the table Marty's man was the last to arrive. The others were quiet until he sat down.

Marty was frightened. He was shaking and afraid. He was scared he would sneeze or shake so much he would make a noise. He crouched down in a tight ball so no one could see him. Finally, he calmed down and listened to what they were saying.

They were planning to pick up a large drug shipment from the docks that night.

They did not stay long. They did want to be seen together. Just as they were about to leave Marty put the camera next to the lattice and snapped a few pictures. He left as soon as the others did. He was relieved to be away from there.

Then Marty thought about what he had witnessed. He could not ignore the fact that a lot of harmful drugs were about to be sold on the streets. He had to do something. His mind was spinning. All he could think of was Detective Banks, so he rode to the police station and asked to speak to him.

"I am Jonnie Eastwood's mate, sir. He's always talking about you. I have come on to some important information that I thought you should know about."

"What could a young lad like you have that would be important?"

"I know that a million dollars' worth of drugs are going to be picked up on the docks tonight. I know where and who the people involved are. Is that important enough?"

Francis just stared at Marty. When he was about to speak Marty said, "I have pictures to prove what I am talking about."

Marty showed Francis the camera.

"Come into my office and you can explain yourself. I must warn you that this better be the truth. We do not like young lads telling us fanciful stories. Give me the camera. I will have the film developed right away."

They sat down at Francis's desk and Marty began talking. He was so excited he could hardly contain himself.

"Calm down, son, and start at the beginning.

"I do odd jobs for Mr St Clare, the lawyer. He wanted me to get some evidence that Jonny Rizzoli was cheating on his wife. I have been following him around for two weeks taking photos of him. Today he changed his routine and sat at a table next to where I was hiding. These other men came in and they talked about a drug shipment that was arriving tonight. They made plans to pick it up."

"That is a very serious thing to say about someone," Francis said. "I will have to check with Mr St Clare to verify your story."

"If you do that, sir, he may inform Jonny Rizzoli. I doubt if you can trust him."

Francis looked at Marty and said, "You are right son and you would not know that about Mr St Clare unless you knew him. Give me all the details about the shipment and when the photos come back, we will take it from there."

Marty told Detective Banks all he had heard. Francis wrote it all down. Just as they finished the office door burst open and another detective came in all excited.

"Francis, these photos are dynamite. They show Jonny and Max Morgan together. The two biggest rival gangs are planning something. We have to find out what it is and stop it before they can organize."

"Calm down, Sam, I already know what is going down. Get the drug squad boys in here, we have a lot to do this afternoon."

When things calmed down Francis said to Marty, "Son, I want to thank you. That was a brave thing you did coming in here with that information. I suggest you stay away from Mr St Clare. If he finds out who gave us the information, he will tell his pal Jonny."

"I think he will be pleased with me, sir. He will get a big fat fee defending Jonny."

Francis laughed then said, "You had better run along before the others arrive. It's better that no one knows who you are."

"May I have my camera back?"

"I'll give it to Mrs Eastwood, you can pick it up there. Thanks again, son, you're a brave boy."

Marty was tingling all over. He was pumped full of adrenalin. He rode to the park doing tricks until he calmed down. He could hardly wait to tell Jonnie of his adventure. He arrived at Jonnie's just as his uncle dropped him off.

"Come with me to the clubhouse. I have something to tell you."

"What did you go to the police for? Especially that Detective Banks. He is very suspicious. I'm sure he wonders about us roaming around at night. What if he figures out that we gave him that other information?"

"Relax, Jonnie, you're more excited than I am. How would you feel if I didn't say anything and all those drugs got on the street?"

You are right Marty I would feel awful each time I read about someone overdosing. You did the right thing."

Marty told Jonnie the whole story and Jonnie was impressed.

"How come you have all the adventures? All I do is work all the time."

"You want some adventure I will give you some if you are brave enough to do it."

"What are you taking about now?"

"I know how we can have some real excitement. Are you game?"

"I'll do anything you will do."

"Okay," Marty said, "we will go to the docks tonight and watch the drug bust."

"What are you crazy? We could get shot or caught and be accused of being an accessory."

"You said you wanted to do something exciting, well here is your chance. We will not get caught. We will go early and climb on top of a stack of containers and watch."

Jonnie thought for a minute then said, "We would be safe on a container and it will be exciting, let's do it."

"Now you're talking. I know where they're going to meet. We will go early and get a good seat."

Marty and Jonnie rode cautiously in the shadows though the dock yard. The yards were large and open; there was traffic there all the time. They rode past warehouse 32, where the pickup was to take place. They found a spot behind some containers to hide their bikes then climbed on to a stack and settled down to wait for the action. They saw some police arrive and position themselves around the warehouse.

All was quiet until a new station wagon came along and parked next to the warehouse. Then a van arrived and parked next to the station wagon.

Soon two men appeared out of nowhere and talked to the others. Then a briefcase appeared and the two men looked in it. Then one of them signalled and a forklift, with a pallet, came out of the shadows. They unloaded the pallet into the van while the two bosses stood talking a little way off.

Suddenly lights came on all around them and a voice called over a loud hailer for them to, "Put your hands on your heads."

The men pulled out their guns and shot at the lights. Then there was shouting and gunfire. A couple men were hit and fell down; another raised his hands. The one with the briefcase ducked behind the van and scurried along the side of the building in the shadows.

Jonnie was all excited watching the action, but Marty kept his eye on the one with the briefcase. Soon it was all over. The police rounded up the men and took some photographs then packed up everything and left.

Marty and Jonnie stayed where they were until they were sure it was safe.

"That was really exciting," Jonnie said, "better than the movies."

They climbed down and picked up their bikes, but when they went to leave Marty went the wrong way.

"Where are you going?" Jonnie asked. "Home is that way."

"I want to look around first," Marty said.

"Come on, before someone sees us."

"It will only take a minute."

Marty rode around the corner, parked his bike against the wall, and walked along, looking at the wall.

"What are you doing? Come on, before someone sees us."

"Jonny Rizzoli sneaked along here with the briefcase," Marty said. "When the cops caught him down there he didn't have it. He hid it along here somewhere. I want to find it."

"What do you want the briefcase for?"

"It's full of money, dummy. Come on, help me find it."

A few minutes later, Marty found a space between two buildings.

"It's in there. I can't reach it. You pull it out."

Jonnie put his long arm into the crack and felt around. "I found it," he said as he pulled it out."

"Great, now let's get out of here."

They rode to the clubhouse to put the briefcase away.

"We'll stash it away until tomorrow," Marty said.

"I want to know how much is in it," Jonnie said.

"It will take us all night to count it and I'm tired."

"We can sleep here. Come on, open it."

Marty and Jonnie sat on a bed counting the money. It took a long time to count one hundred thousand dollars. They were too tired when they finished to be excited. Jonnie slid the briefcase under his bed then laid down and fell asleep. Marty staggered into the next room and dropped on the bed.

CHAPTER TEN

Jonnie could not understand what was happening. He was shaking and someone was calling his name. Freddie was standing over him, shaking him.

"Wake up, Jonnie, we have work to do."

Finally, Jonnie woke up and looked at his uncle. It took a moment for him to realize what was happening.

"I've spent half the morning looking for you. Come On, we're behind schedule."

"Uncle, I'm tired and hungry. You'll have to do it on your own."

"I spent too much time looking for you. I need you to help me."

"We'll take Marty along, that will speed things up. He's in the next room. Wake him up while I get ready."

Marty protested, but it did not do him any good. They were soon at the first shop, tossing drink crates around.

All they had for lunch was a cold pie between stops and it was late when they finished. The boys went home, had their supper and fell in bed.

Marty slept in the next day but Jonnie had to help his uncle. It was the weekend before they got together.

The briefcase was under the bed where Jonnie had left it. They took to the basement and hid it with the other money.

"I've been thinking about what you said about taking chances," Marty said. "We're rich now so we don't have to steal the armoured car."

"That money will set us up for the rest of our life, we are going to do it."

"We already have all we could ever spend," Marty said. "Why take a chance on being caught? We could lose everything."

"There's too much money sitting there waiting for us. We would be silly to pass it up. We will not be caught. The plan is fool proof."

"I suppose you're right," Marty said, "but that will be the last foolhardy thing we do. No more taking chances, no matter how bored we are."

"I agree, we're rich now, we can hire others to do the dangerous things for us."

There was a lot of publicity and news stories about the biggest drug bust ever.

The police rounded up the rest of the men involved and raided their homes and businesses. Two crewmen and the captain of a ship were involved and the police sent all the information to Hong Kong, where more suspects were arrested. Neither Detective Banks or Marty's name was mentioned in any news report. The head of the drug squad took all the credit.

A couple weeks later Francis Banks, who was now a regular at the Eastwood home, was having dinner with Ida and Jonnie. Since Sharon was away, Jonnie ate at home.

When Ida left the table to prepare the dessert, Francis leaned over and spoke quietly to Jonnie. "I have heard a lot about your clubhouse. I would like to see it. Would you mind showing it to me?"

Jonnie stiffened, he was frightened. He paused, then said, "I work all week and Saturday morning. How about Saturday afternoon or Sunday? That's the only free time I have. You could stop by during the day, Marty might be there."

"There's no rush, Saturday afternoon will be fine. I'm just curious, that's all."

"Marty and I will hang around until you arrive."

The next day Jonnie had Freddie drive past the clubhouse in case Marty was there. Jonnie had Freddie stop while he ran inside to tell Marty about the visit.

"He suspects us," Marty said. "I bet he has someone watching us."

"Don't panic, sweep the floor and make sure the money is well hidden. No one suspects a couple of misfits."

Marty spent the afternoon going round checking everything. Then he did it again. When he'd finished, he stood at the office window looking out at the street.

We thought we were too smart, he thought, *now we are going to lose all we have achieved. Detective Banks is a smart cop. He has figured out what happened to the missing briefcase.*

Marty calmed down and walked around the whole clubhouse, making sure everything was perfect.

It is too neat and clean, he thought. *Young guys like us are not neat and clean. He will realize we are hiding something.*

Marty spent the rest of the afternoon making the clubhouse look like two young boys played there.

Saturday morning was easy so Jonnie quit early and found Marty at home. They had a quick lunch then went to the clubhouse.

"We're in big trouble," Marty said. "Detective Banks is on to us. We will spend a long time in jail. We cannot even think of stealing the armoured truck now."

"Calm down, Marty. You're making all this up. We'll jump around on the trampoline and show him a few bike tricks. That's all we do here."

"What if he wants to look downstairs?"

"We'll take him down there. It is just an empty hole. I hope you didn't clean it up."

"No, I messed it up as best I could. It looks like no one has ever been down there. I removed most of the bulbs so it will be very dark if he goes down there."

"Good thinking, now let's practice so we can put on a good show for the crafty detective."

The boys did not notice Francis come in. They were jumping on the trampoline when he came in. He stood watching them and applauded when they finished.

"You guys are good," he said. "You could be in the circus."

"We only do it for fun," Jonnie said. "I have to be careful, my bones are brittle and would not heal well if I broke one of them."

"So, this is your clubhouse, I am amazed. I thought it would be a garage behind Marty's house."

"My uncle found us this place," Jonnie said. "We take care of it for the owner. He wants to build some apartments here but can't raise the money."

"We have to keep to ourselves," Marty added. "We do not like being laughed at."

"I'm not laughing. I think you are good. I think you boys are belittling yourselves. No one will laugh at you."

"Want to bet?" Jonnie said. "Come with us right now to the skateboard ramp and see what happens when we outperform them. You'll have to arrest a couple of them"

"All right, I get the message. I'm sorry I misunderstood."

"We hang around here and keep to ourselves", Marty said. "We like it that way."

"You could join the Police Youth Club and meet others. They have a trampoline."

"I have friends on the basketball team," Jonnie said. "A couple of friends. The others only tolerate me because the team is winning. We're perfectly happy on our own."

"I get the message and I understand. Your mother asked me to check on you. She always worries about you."

"Now you can tell her that I am perfectly normal and happy. Marty and I spend our time here or riding around the park doing tricks on our bikes. Would you like to see a couple of tricks?

The boys put a couple of obstacles in the middle of the room and climbed over them, then did a wheelie and rode backwards.

"That was great. I have to go now. Your mother and I are going dancing tonight, I have to get cleaned up. I almost forgot. Marty, come out to the car with me, I have your camera."

"It's not my camera," Marty said, when he was handed the camera. "It belongs to Mr St Clare. I was taking pictures for him."

"I want you to be careful of him. He is a shifty character."

"We found him in an alley one night. Some thugs had beaten him up. We took him home and patched him up. He has been good to us, he told us to take a business course and go into business for ourselves when we finish school. He said he will advise us. Don't worry, we won't do anything illegal."

"I know that. You came to me instead of telling him about the drug bust. That was a brave thing to do. We stopped the ship at Newcastle and arrested the captain. They found a large amount of illegal cigarettes. The captain claimed he knew nothing about the drugs. Some of his crew were doing that. I have to go, take care of yourself."

"I told you not to worry," Jonnie said after Francis had left. "I think we convinced him we are fair dinkum."

"I hope so, but we will ride around the block from now on before we come in here just to make sure no one is watching us."

"What are we going to do with Mr St Clare's camera?" Jonnie asked. "We should return it."

"We have his private number. Let's call him and make an appointment to see him."

"I have been worried about you boys, come over now and have lunch with me," Mr St Clare said, when they called him.

***

"I could not resist these king prawns. Of course I bought more than I should."

Marty looked at the table set out with plates and silverware and a large bowl of king prawns. Then he looked at Mr St Clare.

"What's going on here? You knew we were coming. Is there anyone else here? There are too many prawns for the three of us."

Jonnie looked at Mr St Clare then quickly looked in the other rooms. He even opened the wardrobe. When he returned he said to Mr St Clare. "Detective Banks questioned us earlier today and now you're treating us to a banquet. We want to know why."

"You boys have been spooked by something. What have you been up to and why would that nosy detective question you? You are the ones who have to answer the questions, not me. I bought these prawns on the way home. I was going to invite you over for supper but you rang so I said, 'Come over now.' I love prawns and could easily eat all of them myself. I have told you my story, now I want you to tell me yours."

"I'm sorry, Mr St Clare," Marty said. "We were coming earlier with the pictures I took but became afraid when we saw the news of the drug bust. The police said they had been watching the gang and I thought they had seen me hanging around the coffee shop. Then the detective came to the clubhouse earlier today. We thought he was going to ask me why I was hanging around the coffee shop."

"He goes with my mother," Jonnie said. "He told us my mother was worried about me so he came to check up on us."

"I can understand why you are upset. No one likes to be questioned by the police. What did you tell him?"

"We didn't say anything," Jonnie said. "We jumped on the trampoline and did a few tricks with our bikes. He seemed to be satisfied with that."

"He wants us to join the Police Youth Club," Marty added.

"Let's hope that is the end of it," Mr St Clare said. "By the way, did you get any evidence on our suspect?"

"When Jonnie told me the detective was coming, I destroyed the film just in case," Marty said. "There wasn't anything on it except Mr Rizzoli and his bodyguards. He was not seeing any woman."

"I suppose you did the right thing. Why are you two so jittery? You are suspicious of everyone."

"We have been picked on all our lives," Jonnie explained. "We are used to being alone and become very suspicious whenever anyone looks at us. It is just natural to us."

"We may be suspicious," Marty added, "but it keeps us out of trouble."

"All right, enough of that, those prawns are waiting to be eaten. We will talk of pleasant things."

The boys only had prawns on special occasions and usually the adults got most of them. These were fat, sweet, delicious prawns. They forgot their worries and ate until they could not eat any more.

Later they sat in the lounge talking. Mr St Clare was bragging about being called by the suspect. "He wants me to defend him, he thinks I can get him off again. There isn't much chance of that because he was caught with the drugs. I would become famous if I found a way to save him from jail."

"I know a way you can do that and become the greatest attorney in the country," Marty said.

Mr St Clare laughed then said, "If you can do that, I will be your personal attorney for the rest of my career."

"I thought you were already going to do that," Jonnie said.

"Yes, I am, but now I will never charge you for my services."

"Will you put that in writing?" Marty asked.

"You fellows are sharp, now tell me what you have in mind."

"Detective Banks was bragging to us about busting the drug ring," Marty said. "He said they arrested the ship captain in Newcastle."

"So, what does that have to do with me becoming a famous attorney?"

"The captain pleaded that he only traded in illegal cigarettes. He did not know about the drugs."

"I don't understand, what have cigarettes got to do with my client?"

"I think you had better hire me as your advisor. Your client went to the docks to pick up a load of cigarettes but was mistaken by the drug runners as their contacts. By the time your client realized what was happening, and could do anything about it, the police moved in."

Mr St Clare sat for a minute then a broad smile slowly grew, then he jumped up, threw his arms in the air and shouted, "I am the greatest attorney in the whole world."

He skipped around the room then came up to Marty, lifted him up and hugged him. "Marty that is sheer genius. Thank you, thank you."

Mr St Clare went to the fridge for some drinks. He sat back in his chair and smiled. "I can see the whole case being played out in the courtroom. I explain the cigarette thing and the judge is calling for order because the prosecutor is shouting at me and the reporters are running for the telephones. Just like in the movies." Then Mr St Clare went quiet. He sat there staring at the far wall.

"What's wrong?" Jonnie said. "Are you all right."

"I will be the most famous attorney ever but I will also be the poorest. My client lost all his money during the drug bust."

"The police will have to return it when he is found innocent," Jonnie said.

"You don't understand, he hid the money when the police arrived but when he went back to retrieve it he couldn't find it. Someone took it. He thinks one of the policemen saw him hiding and came back later and took it. The main suspect is your friend Banks."

Jonnie jumped up and said, "You tell your client to find another suspect. Francis was with my mother that night. I could hear them in the next room when I went to bed."

"Don't get upset, son. I will tell my client what you have told me. I did not think you cared about a policeman."

101

"I don't, it's my mother I'm thinking about. I don't want her upset."

"I will take care of everything. Now this has been a very enlightening afternoon. You boys always liven up my life. What are you going to do next?"

"We're not going to do anything that will get us into trouble," Jonnie said. "We are planning out future and it is looking good. We are going to be successful businessmen and we are not going to do anything dangerous that would interfere with that."

"That is a very noble plan, but remember how you got to this point in your lives. It was not by hiding under the bed. Life is full of dangers. You cannot avoid or hide from them. Remember that. Now, don't be strangers. Come and visit me any time. I am going to spend the next few days preparing my blockbuster case, you will read about it in the papers. Thank you, boys, I will always be in your debt."

Marty and Jonnie rode to the park and did tricks for a while. They sat on a bench then Marty said, "You lied to Mr St Clare; you were not home that night so you do not know if Detective Banks was there."

"You lied too, you did not destroy the film, the cops have it. So we are even. Besides, I know Francis was there. He is there most nights now."

The next morning when Freddie picked up Jonnie, he told him this was his last week as an armoured truck driver.

"My last official job is picking up the old bank notes. Someone else will take them to the incinerator on Saturday morning. I'm going fishing in the Snowy Mountains for two weeks to celebrate."

"What about the drink run, who's going to do that?"

"It will be over this week. We will give everyone a full load to hold them until I return. I may even sell my business. Harold Wilson wants to expand his business. He'll buy my truck and customers for three thousand dollars. I'll get that much from the security company. I can retire."

"Six thousand dollars will not last long, especially if you waste it going fishing."

"The fishing trip will only cost me a little petrol and food. I have a sleeping bag and a camp stove. Besides, I have been offered a job at the hardware store. They want me because I have a lot of experience with machinery and can advise the customers."

"All this is very quick, what are you going to do?"

"I have sold the business and start at the hardware when I return from fishing."

"That was quick, what does Aunt Martha have to say about all of this."

"She doesn't care where the money comes from as long as it comes in and she doesn't want me hanging around the house all day."

Later that day, Jonnie told Marty what was happening.

"We're ready," Marty said. "We will tell our mothers that we're sleeping at each other's houses then leave from the clubhouse early in the morning. It will only take fifteen minutes."

"We'll have a practice session on Friday afternoon," Jonnie said.

"What about Detective Banks, what if he becomes suspicious?"

"Don't worry about him. He's only interested in my mother. She wouldn't like it if she thought he was spying on me. Besides, we haven't seen anyone lurking around the clubhouse. Relax, all is well."

CHAPTER ELEVEN

When Ida came home after work on Wednesday, she sat Jonnie down and told him she had something important to tell him.

"As you know, dear, Francis has been seeing a lot of me. I hope you understand. I am still young and he is a kind, gentle man. I like him very much. What I want to say is... Well, Francis has a week off so we have decided to go away so we can be alone and get to know each other better. I think he is going to ask me to marry him. I want to know how you feel about that and Francis. I hope you understand."

"Mother, I have been expecting this. I like Francis. I want you to be happy but I won't put up with him if he tries to order me around. I have my life all planned out and I don't want anyone interfering with my plans. He is marrying you, not me. As long as he leaves me alone, I will agree with you. I want you to be happy. I can remember how you used to cry a lot. If Francis makes you happy, that's all that matters."

"I know Francis is a good man and he's only thinking of your welfare. I'm sure he won't try to control you."

"Mother, Francis doesn't know me. He compares me with other normal boys and wants me to be like them. I'm not normal and can't be like other boys. I know and understand that. I'm planning a good life for Marty and me. We're going to study business management and start our own business. We know we can't do ordinary work and we don't like being around people. They stare and laugh at us. I don't want anyone trying to change me."

"Jonnie, dear, you have to accept certain things in your life. There are things you cannot change. People will always laugh at you, there is nothing you can do about it."

"I know that, Mother, but there is something I can do about it. I can minimise it by keeping away from people. It hurts when they make fun of me. I am keeping the hurt down to as little as possible. So far I have done very well. I like my life and will not let anyone change it. You can tell that to your future husband."

Jonnie picked up his skateboard and left. He rode around until supper time. He knew he had to face Francis some time and he was hungry.

After supper, instead of helping Ida with the dishes, Francis asked Jonnie to go for a walk with him.

"I want to know how you feel if your mother and I got married," Francis said as they walked around the block.

"My mother likes you and I am sure you will be good to her. I want my mother to be happy and if marrying you makes her happy, I will not object."

"Thank you, Jonnie, I am as lonely as your mother and we need each other. We both are tired of being lonely. I will do my best to make her happy, you can be assured of that."

"There is one condition to this marriage," Jonnie said. "As I told my mother, I have my life all planned out and I don't want you interfering with my plans. You are marrying my mother, not me."

"Jonnie, you are only seventeen, how can you plan your whole life out so soon?"

"You have not lived my life and experienced the things I have. If I try to live like others, I will be having bad experiences all my life. I am peaceful and happy now and have formed a plan to stay that way. It does not include trying to be a normal person."

"Jonnie, you have to live in the real world. You can't make up your own fanciful one."

"I will get my skateboard and we will go over to the ramp and I will try to be a normal boy. What do you think will happen?"

"All right. Tell me what your plans are, so I will be better able to understand you."

"Our plans are simple. Marty and I are going to study business management next year and when we leave high school, start our own business. We know we can never get a good job in the real world so we are going to make our own jobs."

"Jonnie, that is brilliant. Marty told me something like that the other day. I thought he was just making it up to impress me. I did not realize you had thought things out so well. I thought you had some fanciful dream, but you are being very practical. I am proud of you."

"Thank you, I thought you would try to make me into a normal boy. You know very well that would fail and I would be miserable. I have learned how to take care of myself. Marty and I have talked this over many times. We're going to take the next year to find out what we like and plan from there. I know we will be successful. We have to be."

"I have something else to tell you now that will affect your life. I am going to ask your mother to marry me and then I am going to apply for a promotion. I will no longer be a detective I will have a desk job and come home every day at the same time."

"Congratulations, we are both planning better lives for ourselves."

"There is one problem; it means a move to another command. I will most probably have to move to Wollongong or Newcastle. You will have to move with us."

Jonnie looked straight into Francis's eyes and said, "I told you, I will not change my life. I am staying here with Marty. We are going to graduate from high school then go to business college or tech school. After you marry my mother you can take her anywhere you want to, but I am not included in your plans."

Francis had to step back. He could feel the resentment coming from Jonnie. He composed himself and said cautiously, "I'm sorry you've taken it so hard. You can study anywhere. I am sure your mother wants you with her."

"I love my mother dearly and I know that she would be a lot happier with me out of her life. She has put up with a lot because of me. It cost her a marriage and she very seldom ever took me anywhere. I know she was embarrassed when people looked at me. She will be much happier without me around."

Francis was stunned. He did not realize how deeply Jonnie was hurting until he let it all out. He could not answer. He knew Jonnie was right. Ida did not invite him for dinner until he'd met Jonnie. Now he knew why. The family hurt ran deep.

"Jonnie, I have no answer for what you have said. It will be at a least a year before I have to move. By then we should have a better idea of what is going to happen. Let's leave it at that. I will not force you to do anything you don't want to do. I want us to be a happy loving family. None of us have had that, so let's try to find it with our new life."

Francis held out his hand. Jonnie shook it then they hugged. They did not speak on the way home.

The next morning at breakfast Ida had a serious talk with her son. "Jonnie, do you really understand what is going on? Francis and I are making plans to marry. Do you understand what that means? If you have any doubts or misgivings about it, I want to know now. I will not go through with it if you do not approve."

"Mother, I want you to be happy. Francis is a good man. He told me he will do his best to make you happy. I told him how I feel. As long as he doesn't interfere with my plans, I'll go along with your plans. I want you to be happy. You don't have to worry about me. I'm as happy and well-adjusted as a boy like me can be. Have a good time and fall in love and be happy."

"Thank you, Jonnie, I am proud of you."

They hugged and Ida kissed her son on the forehead. Jonnie was pleased. He could not remember the last time his mother kissed him.

"Try to come back for lunch, dear, I'm coming home then and we're leaving early this afternoon. I want to say goodbye. I have made arrangements with Mrs McAlister. You are going to stay there while we're away."

"Mother, you didn't have to do that. I can take care of myself. I will be fine on my own."

"This is just in case something happens. I would be in trouble if something happened to you if I left you on your own."

"All right, I'll be fine, I've stayed there before."

"I have made a large meat loaf to take with you. Come back at lunch time."

***

After a delicious meat loaf meal, Marty and Jonnie went riding.

"We'll have to rearrange our plans," Jonnie said. "We had planned to tell our parents that we would be at each other's house. How are we going to get away tomorrow night?"

"If we can't sneak out of the house without my parents hearing us, we might as well forget the whole idea. We only need your bike. We'll leave it at the clubhouse. We'll only be away for a half hour at the most."

"I'm just getting excited. Up to now it has just been planning but now it's going to really happen. Are you excited?"

"I will be excited when it is over. This has to be perfect. The girls are coming home this weekend. We have to have everything finished by Saturday afternoon."

"I forgot about the girls," Jonnie said. "They have been gone for so long. We have to retrieve the invoices from the sacks and mail them right away, otherwise the government will come looking for them."

"Now you're worrying, relax, everything will work out."

Around one in the morning, Marty was shaking Jonnie, trying to wake him up. Jonnie slipped out of the window then helped Marty out. They trotted to the clubhouse then rode to the security building on Jonnie's bike.

The operation went smoothly and they were soon on their way home to Marty's house. Jonnie pushed Marty in the window then climbed in behind him. The next thing Jonnie knew Marty was shaking him.

"Wake up, Jonnie, we have a lot to do today."

They tried to be casual at breakfast. The talk was about the girls returning. Gloria and her family would arrive on the boat from Tasmania late in the afternoon and Sharon would arrive on the bus tomorrow morning.

The boys went straight to the clubhouse then down to the basement. They pulled the bags from the truck and lined them up next to the bench.

"How are we going to get the locks off? Jonnie asked.

"I bought a bolt cutter from the hardware store," Marty said. "That should do it."

The padlocks were small but made of hardened steel. They could not cut them.

"We have to do this today," Jonnie said. "It's the only time we have."

"I'll get the hacksaw from upstairs," Marty said. "That will do it."

They put a padlock in the vice and started sawing. It worked, but it was slow.

"This will take all day," Jonnie said. "Besides, the blade won't last long. Freddie has a small angle grinder. You keep cutting while I go get it."

Marty had two locks cut when Jonnie returned. "That was hard work," Marty said. "The blade is dull all ready."

"The angle grinder will fix it," Jonnie said. "We'll have it done in no time."

Jonnie was right. The angle grinder ate through the locks with ease.

Jonnie had watched the supervisor at the incinerator so he knew what to do with the paperwork. He soon had the envelope ready to mail.

"What are we going to do with the bags?" Marty asked.

"I had forgotten about them. We'll box them up and put them with a load of trash. Freddie will dump them in the incinerator when he comes back."

"Can we trust him to do that?"

"I will load them on the truck and go to the incinerator with him and personally toss them into the fire."

The only place to store the money bags was under the bench, there were so many of them. They lined them up then quit for the day. It was well after lunch time. They were hungry and exhausted.

The boys dropped the letter into a mailbox then bought a pizza, rode to the park and sat under a tree relaxing and eating pizza.

Later Marty washed and changed his clothes then rode to Gloria's house to greet her. They were already there. Gloria ran up to Marty and hugged him.

"I looked for you as soon as we came into town," Gloria said. "I thought you had forgotten me."

"We've been talking about you all day. I didn't know what time you would arrive."

"I'm glad to know that you didn't forget me. I'm very tired from the trip. Come by tomorrow afternoon when I'm rested. I'm glad to be home and extra glad to see you. Until tomorrow."

Gloria gave Marty a peck on the cheek and went into the house. He was slightly annoyed, but relieved. He was worn out too. He and Jonnie spent the evening watching television. They looked at every news channel for news about the security company. Not a word on any channel.

"I think we did it," Jonnie said.

Sharon rode all night on the bus. She arrived early in the morning then came home on the train. She did not travel well, so she laid down and slept most of the day,

Marty and Jonnie went to the clubhouse right after breakfast. They were eager to count the money. They soon realized it was going to be a long slow process.

They thought the money would be counted and in bundles. It was tossed in the bag. All different denominations and condition. Some bills were in poor condition. Worn out and dirty. Others had small tears or were wrinkled. They had to examine each one. It took all morning to do one bag.

"This is going to take forever," Marty said.

"So what, we have plenty of time. We can't spend any of this until we start our business."

"What are we going to do with the notes we can't use?"

"We'll dump them in the incinerator with the bags."

When they finished, they had piles of notes arranged on the table.

"We forgot to get some rubber bands to tie them up," Marty said. "What are we going to do with them.?"

"We have some plastic shopping bags leftover from the brothel files," Jonnie said. "Put each type in a different bag."

There were lots of one and two-dollar notes. They took a couple of bags each. There was a bag each of five and ten-dollar notes, but only a few twenty and fifty-dollar ones.

"I don't think we're going to have as much money as we thought if the rest of the bags are like this one," Marty said. "How are we going to spend all these one and two-dollar bills?"

"What's wrong with you today? All you're doing is complaining. We're rich, be happy. Here, take a few one-dollar notes and spend them. That will get rid of them."

"We have to be careful so no one will notice us."

"No one pays attention to a kid spending a dollar. If you were flashing fifty-dollar notes, they would wonder where you got them."

The boys put everything away and went home for lunch.

After lunch, Marty went to visit Gloria and Jonnie stopped at Sharon's house. They were soon home again, disillusioned and looking for something to do.

"Sharon is worn out from her log trip," her father said. "She's sleeping. Come back tomorrow."

Gloria came to the door. She told Marty she was seasick from the boat trip.

"I hope I'm better tomorrow," she said.

The boys spent the rest of the day watching videos.

***

There was only a week left before school started again. Marty and Jonnie did not have anything to do but count money. They decided they would do one bag a day.

Marty was getting disappointed. The one and two-dollar notes were stacking up.

"Relax," Jonnie said, "we will find a way to get rid of them."

"We can't go into a store and buy something with bags of one and two-dollar notes."

Marty stopped at Gloria's house but no one was home. Jonnie sat on the lounge with Sharon. She was not very talkative and declined to go to the movies or for a walk. Jonnie left wondering what was happening.

Jonnie found Sharon tossing baskets when he rode into her yard the next day.

"I'm sorry about yesterday," Sharon said. "I'm not a good traveller. I couldn't sleep on the bus. It stopped in every town. I feel better today."

They tossed a few baskets then sat down and talked.

"I had a great time," Sharon said. "My cousin has a boyfriend so we double dated with his mate. He has a car. We went to the beach and a concert. It was fun."

"I'm sorry, Sharon, I don't have a rich father who can buy me a car. I don't even have a job any more because my uncle sold his truck. All I can be is a good friend."

"Jonnie, you're a nice guy and I like you but we never do anything. You won't go anywhere except to the movies. I had a great time this summer and I am going to have fun and go out and do things. I was shy before but now I realize that people only look for a minute. A couple of senior boys asked me for a date last year and I declined. This year I am going out and having fun. You're nice but you're dull. I want to live and enjoy life.

Jonnie was stunned. He was quiet then said, "I can understand what you're saying. I can't compete with boys with cars and money. I may be dull but I'm planning for my future. I am going to be a successful businessman and have a good life. I can't waste the money I don't have on fun things. I'm sorry that you want more, but I understand."

"Jonnie, that's what's wrong with you. All you talk about is how successful you're going to be. You're only young once. Go out and have some fun."

"It costs money to have fun. I don't have any money. Go have your fun, but when you look back in a few years you will only remember the wonderful time you and I had at the school ball. When you're broke and roaming the streets, come and see me in my big office at my successful business. I'll give you a job for old times' sake."

Jonnie stood up jumped on his bike and said, "See you around," as he rode off. Sharon tried to shrug it off but deep down she realized that he was right.

Much the same happened to Marty. He finally caught up with Gloria. They went for a walk and ended up sitting on a bench in the park.

"You've been very quiet since you returned. Did something happen to you while you were away?"

"No, Marty, I had a great time. I'm sorry I didn't write as often as I said I would. I have something to tell you but I don't know how to say it."

"The only thing to do is tell me. I'll understand."

"What I have to say is going to hurt you and I don't want to hurt you."

"You will hurt me a lot more if you don't tell me."

"All right, Marty, I'm not going back to school this year."

"What do you mean? You have to finish school. You're going to go into business with Jonnie and me."

"Marty, that's what I'm trying to tell you. I won't be going in business with you. I'm going to Tasmania."

Marty looked at Gloria then said, "I don't understand, we made plans."

"My parents are moving to Tasmania very soon. My father is going into business with his brother. Marty, we're too young to be making plans for the future. I don't want to be stuck in an office all my life. My cousin goes to a dance academy down there. I went with her one day. They teach acrobatic dancing. The principal told me I was really talented and could get a good job in the movies and on the stage. I want to be somebody, not an office clerk."

"Gloria, you're making plans just the same as I am. Doing the same routine night after night on the stage is not much fun. Think about it."

"I'm sorry, Marty, I like you a lot, but I have dreams too. Maybe when we grow up we'll meet again and take up again. But now my life has changed and I'm changing with it. I won't forget you. I'll write to you."

They walked back to Gloria's house without speaking and Gloria ran into the house without saying goodbye.

That evening, Marty and Jonnie sat under their favourite tree in the park. They were gloomy and despondent. "When we started the school holiday everything was great," Jonnie said. "Now a month later it's a mess. The girls are gone, I don't have a job any more and my mother is getting married and moving away. All our great plans have gone up in smoke."

They sat there for a while then Marty spoke. "Nothing has changed. Other people have changed but we haven't. We still have our grand plan and nothing is going to interfere with it. If others don't want to be part of our life then they can go their own way. Nothing is going to stop us from being successful."

"You're right, Marty. That's what I told my mother and her future husband. 'You're marrying each other, not me.' We fell for the girls but they weren't really interested in us. Marty, it's only you and I. We have our plan and we are going to be successful We need each other to fulfil that plan. You and me, Marty, now and forever."

"You and me, Jonnie, nothing and no one will interfere with the grand plan."

They sat there for a long time thinking about what had happened. Jonnie finally broke the silence. "I really don't miss Sharon. I had almost forgotten her. She didn't write all the time she was away and didn't think about me, so why should I worry about her."

"Gloria was different, she wasn't the same person. I won't have any trouble forgetting her."

It was getting late. The boys stood up, then Jonnie said, "You and I, Marty, just you and I. We are going to be successful and rich. Nothing and no one is going to stop us."

"You're right, Jonnie, we will not fail."

CHAPTER TWELVE

School started on Tuesday but the teachers were there on Monday preparing for the opening. Marty and Jonnie went to the school on Monday to talk to the councillor.

She was pleasantly surprised to have two students who were thinking about the future. She set up a new course for them.

"You do realize that this is a much harder curriculum than what you were used to. You will have to study and keep up with the class in order to graduate."

"This is our future," Jonnie said. "We have to succeed."

"I wish all the students had your attitude. Call on me any time. I'm here to help you."

Marty and Jonnie realized right away that school would be different. They were in a different part of the building. They did not know anyone. It was like a different school. They did not know any of the teachers or the students.

The boys received another shock. The first day they had an assignment and homework. Neither of them had ever done any studying. The first two weeks were tough, until they were used to the new routine.

They had a goal so they buckled down and worked hard. If there was a difficult assignment, they both worked on it. They tried to turn in different papers so the teacher would not accuse them of copying.

By the end of the first term they were near the top of the class.

The basketball team had a new coach who did not like the way Jonnie played so he quit. He did not have time to practice anyway. Also there was not much time to ride around doing tricks. They set up a study room in the office at the clubhouse. That is the only time they were there. They wanted to watch over their money.

In their spare time they finished counting the money. There wasn't as much there as they thought would be. Only three hundred and fifty thousand dollars. They did not realize there would be so many small bills.

Another problem that they did not figure on was, Freddie sold his truck. They had boxes of old bills and money bags to dispose of and no way to do it.

By the half year mark the boys had converted themselves to real students who were doing well in their studies.

At least once a week they would visit Mr St Clare and discuss various businesses. They were learning. They could carry on a conversation with him. Jonnie was interested in the stock market. Mr St Clare gave him a book outlining the procedures of the market. He was following one of the editors of the financial page in the daily paper. Marty was learning about the real estate market. Whenever a property was put up for sale in the area he would follow the procedure until it was sold. He became known to the local agents.

With all their schoolwork and studying there wasn't much time to ride around doing tricks. Sometimes on a Sunday morning they would go to the skateboard ramp and then ride around the park. They were slowly becoming adults and they no longer tried to learn any new tricks. The boys had a full schedule with little spare time. When the mid tern vacation started their routine changed. Jonnie's mother was married and the boys had a job.

Francis and Ida decided to marry after spending a week away. They realized then they were lonely and needed each other. They set the date for June during the school holidays. Francis applied for a promotion and it came through quicker than he thought it would. There had been more retirements than were expected.

Francis would have a senior position in the personnel department, placing the right people in the right area. The one problem was he had to train for the new job. Normally he could do it on his own time but that would take over a year. The department wanted him right away. He would have to study full time for six months at Wollongong University. Ida wanted to go with him, but there was Jonnie. They spent a lot of time talking about it but could not decide what to do. They knew Jonnie would not go with them. Ida could not afford the rent without a job and paying two rents would be a strain on Francis. They decided to talk to Jonnie.

"I don't know what you two are so upset about," Jonnie said. "Give up the flat and move to Wollongong. I can take care of myself."

"You have to have a place to live and buy your own food," his mother said. "How are you going to do that?"

"I have a place to live and I have a job. Come on, I'll show you. It will be quicker than trying to explain it to you."

Jonnie took them to the clubhouse. His mother had never been there. He showed them around then took them upstairs. He showed them the study room. There were books and papers on the desk and two white boards, one by each desk.

"Marty and I study here each afternoon. We don' have any time to use the gym equipment so we're going to sell it. That will give us some extra money. Now to show you the main attraction."

Jonnie led them into the flat. They were pleasantly surprised. It was well furnished and neat and clean.

"Marty and I will live here. We spend most of our time here anyway, studying."

Ida and Francis looked around and realized that Jonnie could easily take care of himself here."

"It will cost you a lot of money to live here, especially when you have to buy food."

"I have figured that out. The man who bought uncle's courier business wants to store things here. He is going to pay half of the rent. We're already were paying the rent so that half will pay for the food. Also we're working for him two afternoons a week and on Saturdays. We will be fine. We don't have time to play here any more so we will sell the gym equipment and have a kitty for emergencies. If I get short, I will give you a yell. You don't have to worry about me. You can see I have figured everything out."

"You have eased my worries," his mother said, "but what will happen when your school mates come here for their parties?"

"Mother, you worry too much. Marty and I have been here for two years. Other than Uncle Freddie and Mr Wilson—he is the courier operator—you and Francis are the only other people that have been in here." Of course, Jonnie did not mention the girls. "You can make your plans to go to Wollongong. I'll come down for the wedding."

Ida hugged her son, kissed him on the cheek. "Thank you, Jonnie, you are all grown up so I don't have to worry about you any more. I'll pay to have a telephone installed here so we can keep in touch. You've made me very happy."

Francis shook Jonnie's hand. "Thank you, son. I wasn't sure about you when we first met. Now I know you can take care of yourself."

Ida and Francis went away happy and began planning their move to Wollongong.

Jonnie could not wait to tell Marty.

***

One afternoon after school Marty and Jonnie had arrived at the clubhouse to find Freddie's truck parked at the back gate. A man got out as they approached.

"You must be Jonnie," he said. "I'm Harold Wilson, a mate of Freddie. He told me about you. He said you were good dependable workers. The business has grown. I need some help so I was wondering if you two would like to earn some spending money."

"We're always short of money, Mr Wilson but we don't have any spare time," Jonnie said. "Our schoolwork keeps us busy."

"I need you two afternoons after school and most of Saturday. I'll pay you more than Freddie did."

"What do you think, Marty? We could use the money."

"I don't know. Can we talk about it?"

"Would you excuse us for a couple of minutes, Mr Wilson while we discuss this?"

Mr Wilson smiled, then sat in his truck.

"Our life is complicated enough now," Marty said. "Why add to it?"

"I've been trying to think of a way to get rid of our trash," Jonnie said. "This is a good way to do it. When we can trust him, we will have him take the trash to the incinerator for us."

"That's a good idea, but what if he decides to look in the boxes?"

"We'll do it on a day we're working with him and go to the incinerator with him."

"All right, having a job will allow us to spend some money too."

Jonnie opened the door of the truck and said, "We will work for you, Mr Wilson, but it can only be two afternoons and Saturday. We have to keep up with our schoolwork."

"You will be a big help, what days do you want to work?"

"Our easiest days are Tuesday and Wednesday. We can leave school at lunch time on Wednesday. That's sport day and we don't do sport."

"That works right in with my schedule. Wednesday is my busiest day. You can start on Saturday I'll pick you up here at eight o'clock. We should be done by noon. Thank you, boys, I'm sure we'll get along."

Mr Wilson drove off and Marty and Jonnie went inside to talk about their new job.

"We're doing well in school," Marty said, "so the job won't interfere with our studies."

"We're going to get rid of the trash," Jonnie added. "That was bothering me. Another bonus is you'll be paid too. You used to work for free with Freddie."

Marty and Jonnie liked working for Mr Wilson. He was easy to get along with and he paid them twenty-five dollars each a week. That gave them an excuse to spend some of the money they had.'

There was a reason Mr Wilson asked the boys to work for him. He did need their help but he also needed a warehouse to store the goods he traded. When they got to know each other, he asked the boys the big question.

"Freddie told me about your clubhouse. He said he used to keep his truck there and store things there too. I was wondering if I could make the same arrangement with you? I need somewhere to store the goods I buy. I sometimes clean out houses when people move. I sell the stuff to other dealers but sometimes I have to store it until someone wants it. There isn't much room where I live."

"I suppose so," Jonnie said, "but there a few rules. I am sure Freddie told you that we're loners. We have the clubhouse as a refuge from people because they laugh at us. If we allow you to use it for storage, you have to solemnly promise not to take anyone there to show them your goods. We don't want anyone to know where we hang out. We would have to move once they found us."

"Surly you're exaggerating. No one is that cruel."

"Mr Wilson, you are normal," Marty said. "You have no idea what Jonnie and I have experienced. The only public place we go to is school, otherwise we spend our time in the clubhouse."

"We used to have a gym there," Jonnie added, "but we don't have time to exercise now. We study there now."

"Pay more attention when we're working with you," Marty said. "Listen to the wisecracks we get from people passing by."

"Especially the street gangs," Jonnie added. "They're always looking for someone to fight with. If we answered back to them, they would never leave us alone."

"Once they found out where we hung out, we wouldn't be safe here any more," Marty added.

"I'm sorry, boys I didn't realize you had it so tough. You appear to be happy, well-adjusted boys. I will never tell anyone where you hang out or bring anyone here. You can depend on me. Also, I will pay you rent for the use of the storage space."

"All right, sir," Jonnie said, "we will show you around on Saturday. We have a favour to ask of you too. There is some trash there we want to get rid of. We will help you move it."

"We have some gym equipment to sell too," Marty added. "You can sell that for us."

"I know a mate who deals in gym equipment, it will be easy to sell."

The next afternoon the boys moved the boxes of old money and bags upstairs and packed them in a corner with some other trash they had. They made it look like it had been there for a long time.

They quit early on Saturday. Mr Wilson bought them a pie for lunch then they drove to the clubhouse.

Harold was impressed with the size of the building. The boys showed them the pile of boxes.

"That is only one load," Harold said. "We can take that away now. The incinerator is open until four. I thought you said you some gym equipment," he continued. "All that is here is a big trampoline."

"The rest is upstairs," Jonnie said. "We used the open space to do tricks on our bikes."

"This is a better equipped gym than the one my mate has. He will be pleased to get this. You will get a good price for all of this and I know he will want that large trampoline. I wish I could show this to him but I will keep my promise. We'll plan to move it next Tuesday."

While they were there, Marty jumped up to the rings and went through his routine, ending up with an iron cross. Mr Wilson was amazed.

"You are good," he said, "just like an Olympian."

"We had lots of time to practise. Come downstairs, we'll show you what we can do on the trampoline."

When they finished, Mr Wilson applauded.

"That was wonderful. Why do you want to sell your equipment? I can see you enjoy what you are doing."

"We should not be doing this any more," Jonnie said, "because we don't have the time to practise."

"If you don't continuously practice you can be badly hurt," Marty added, "so we have to give it up."

"It is a shame because you are good."

"We only do it for our own pleasure," Jonnie said. "We could never make a career out of it. "

"Why not? I have never seen anyone as good as you two are."

"There are thousands out there who are just as good or better than we are," Marty said.

"If we hurt ourselves, we would be out of work," Jonnie added. "We're studying hard to learn a trade that will pay well and not break our bones."

"It was fun," Marty said, "but we have to move on."

"Suppose you boys know what you're doing. We'd better get this trash loaded if we want to be at the incinerator by four."

Jonnie stood on the tray of the truck and tossed the last box in the hopper. He signalled the operator and smiled when the hopper tilted up and the boxes slid into the fire. A great worry had been lifted from him.

***

It took all Tuesday afternoon to load the gym equipment and then unload it at the new location. They were tired when they finished.

"You boys did all right," Harold said. "I got five hundred for all of that. "

"That is good," Jonnie said. "That's about what we paid for it. You keep a hundred for your share."

"You don't have to do that, I'm glad to help you and you're doing me a favour too."

"We insist," Marty added, "that is a big hurdle out of the way."

"I will buy a takeaway Chinese. You can come to my place for supper."

"You're on," Marty said, "I love Chinese food."

Marty and Jonnie were surprised when Harold pulled into his driveway. He lived in the biggest house in the best area of Alexandria. The inside of the house was spacious, neat and clean and had some expensive furnishings."

"I didn't know the second-hand business paid so well," Jonnie said, as he looked around

"This was my parents' home," Harold said. "my father was a banker. I was an accountant but gave it up years ago. I had high blood pressure and was sick all the time. Being outside and moving around cured me. Some of the furnishings came with the house, others I picked up cleaning out houses. I do all right but the business got too big for me. You boys are a big help and I am grateful."

"What are you going to do when we leave school and start our own business?" Marty asked.

"I was going to quit if you boys would not work for me. I will sell this place and retire to a North Coast retirement village."

"What do you want to do that for?" Marty asked. "Stay here and be our accountant. We plan to have a large, successful business."

Harold laughed and said, "You boys have big plans. What kind of business are you going into?"

"We don't know yet," Jonnie said. "I'm looking at the stock market and Marty likes real estate."

"We're doing the business course in high school and later we'll go to tech when we decide what we want to do," Marty added.

"I know you will be successful," Harold said, "but I don't think I will be around that long. It will take you years to build up your business."

"It won't take long," Jonnie said. "We have already figured it out. All we have to decide on is what kind of business to go into."

"Maybe you could advise us on what type of business to go into," Marty said.

"The only advice I will give you right now is to stay away from banks and big companies. Stay small and lean. Keep all your money and try not to borrow."

"That's what we plan to do," Jonnie said. "We're saving our money and hope to have enough to start without borrowing any."

"You'll have to make a lot more than fifty dollars a week if that's what you are planning. It will take ten thousand to open a real estate office and at least fifty thousand to buy a seat on the stock exchange."

"That's about what we figured," Marty said. "We're on track to do that."

"You boys are amazing. Come on, I'll take you home."

On the way they had to tell Harold they were living in the clubhouse. It took a few minutes to explain the situation to him.

CHAPTER THIRTEEN

Occasionally Jonnie would see Sharon at school, mostly passing in the corridor between classes. She was hanging around with a group of girls who hung around with the football players. She was easy to spot because he and her were a head taller than the other students. Sharon would not look at Jonnie when they passed. She would lean down, pretending she was talking with the girls. A couple of times after school he saw her get in a car with a senior football player.

One day when Jonnie went to his locker, he passed the girls playing basketball. He stood back out of sight to watch Sharon. She wasn't very good. She had lost the enthusiasm she had. She appeared to be bored and not interested in the game.

Now and then Jonnie and Marty had different classes. One lunch time Jonnie was eating alone. He looked around the cafeteria and saw Sharon eating alone. She looked sad. He decided to sit with her.

"Hi, Sharon, mind if I sit with you?'

Sharon was surprised to see Jonnie. She smiled slightly and moved to the next seat so he could sit down. "Nice to see you, Jonnie, you're looking well. Where's Marty?"

"We has different classes on Thursday. I'll meet him after school. Where are your friends?"

"What friends? I went out with Joyce's boyfriend. She's the unofficial leader of the pack, I have been blackballed. He lied and told me they had broken up. Because I was a member of the snobbies, none of the other girls will talk to me now."

"I didn't realize such silly things went on in school."

"Of course not, you only hang around with Marty. Gloria is gone so I'm all alone now."

"It can't be that bad, it won't take long before some of the other girls socialise with you."

"You're a dreamer, Jonnie. It has been two weeks and no one has spoken to me until you did."

"I am sorry, Sharon, I don't know what to say."

"Say hi to me when we pass in the corridor. At least someone knows I go to school here."

The bell rang, Sharon stood up, said, "See you around Jonnie," and walked off.

"There goes one sad girl," Jonnie thought. He tried to feel sorry for her, but he told himself she brought it on herself."

Because Marty was living with Jonnie, his parents insisted that they have dinner with them every Sunday so they could keep in touch with their son. They were very reluctant at first but, after a little persuasion and the promise to keep up with his studies, they agreed. This Sunday they were going to visit a relative so Jonnie was on his own. He thought of Sharon and decided to stop and say hi.

"Marty, how nice to see you," Sharon's father said. "We're about to have lunch. Come and join us."

"I don't want to be a bother. I just come by to say hi to Sharon."

"Thank you, Jonnie," Sharon said, "come and join us."

"Tell us what you have been doing," Sharon's mother said.

"Marty and I are taking a business course at school. It's hard so we spend a lot of time studying. When we're not studying we have a part time job two afternoons a week and all day Saturday."

"You are busy," Sharon's father said. "When do you have time to practice basketball?"

"I quit basketball. The new coach wanted me to run up and down the court with the other players. I can't do that so I quit."

"He's coaching the girls' team too," Sharon said. "I quit for the same reason. No one likes him."

After lunch Sharon and Jonnie went outside. They tossed a few baskets then sat and talked.

"It was nice of you to come by. I thought you had forgotten about me."

"Sharon, you left me. I didn't walk out on you. Right now, you know who your real friends are."

"I am sorry, Jonnie, I thought my life was boring but I was wrong. I wanted to come by the clubhouse but

I thought you wouldn't speak to me. I soon realized the exciting life was not all that it appeared to be. The girls talk about each other behind their backs and it is very expensive hanging around with them. All their boyfriends want to do is get them in bed. I'm glad to be free of them but I miss Gloria. She was a true friend and I treated her badly."

"I suppose she's going through the same experience in Tasmania. She said she would write to Marty but she never has. Marty can't write to her because he doesn't have her address."

"She wrote to me once, if Marty wants the address I'll give it to him."

"I'll tell him, but I think he's forgotten her."

"Have you forgotten me?"

"I should be asking you that, remember you left me."

"I'm sorry, Jonnie, after the good time I had up north, I wanted more of it when I came back. You have to admit you and Marty are boring."

Jonnie smiled. "Sharon, we don't have rich parents and you have to admit we bring out the worst in people. There are always stories in the papers about people being attacked by roving gangs. We don't want to be attacked and we're smart enough to know all we have to do is be in a crowd. Someone will tease us and that will lead to a fight."

"I've been teased but that's all that has ever happened."

"One day you'll meet a gang of street girls, then you'll find out the hard way what I'm trying to tell you."

"Let's talk about something pleasant. Will you come and visit me again?"

"I have a very tight schedule. There's only Saturday afternoon and Sunday. I don't have a car, so I'm not much fun."

"Don't be so negative. We can find things to do."

"You think of something to do and we will do it. Remember, no crowds."

"There must be something we can do other than shooting baskets."

"Can you ride a skateboard? I can teach you how to do that."

"I always wanted to do that but I'm afraid to fall off."

"I'll give you your first lesson now. You can practice all week and be ready to ride next week."

"Great, but I don't have a skateboard."

"I have plenty of them. One for every day of the week."

Jonnie found a board and a piece of pipe and showed Sharon how to balance on it.

"First you learn to balance, then roll back and forth like this. If you can do that by next weekend, you'll be ready to ride."

"That's easy, I can do that right now."

Sharon soon learned that it was not as easy as it looked.

"I'll practice all week."

Jonnie was invited to stay for supper, then they watched a program on television. "Don't be a stranger," Sharon's mother said when he left.

Sharon walked him to the footpath. They kissed, then Sharon said, "See you on Thursday."

Jonnie was walking along the dark street thinking about Sharon and trying to make sense of the afternoon when a car slowly drove past him. A young man stuck his head out the window and called out, "Hey, scarecrow, get a life."

They all laughed and Jonnie ignored them until the car stopped a little ways up the street. Jonnie did not hesitate. He jumped over a fence, ran through someone's yard, out their back gate and down the lane.

He couldn't run very fast so he stayed in the shadows. If he saw a car coming he would hide in the shadows. When he arrived home, Marty was there.

"Where have you been? I was getting worried."

Jonnie had to tell Marty about his afternoon with Sharon.

"I feel sorry for Sharon," Marty said. "I wonder if Gloria is going through the same thing."

"You can write to her, Sharon has her address."

"I'll let Sharon write and tell her that she has seen us. You be careful with Sharon. She's sad and lonely right now. As soon as a boy comes along in a car she'll drop you and ride away."

"I was wondering about that too. I'll be her friend for now. She needs a friend."

"Yes, she does," Marty said, "one with a car."

"We can get a car. I can get my license through the school driving programme."

"Get your license, but we're not going to waste our money on a car just to take a girl on a date."

"We have to have some social life."

***

The boys had a post office box. It came with the business registration. Jonnie had Harold apply for a telephone; he thought a technician would have to install it.

"You have three phone outlets already, in the office, the kitchen and the bedroom," Harold told them. "All you have to do is buy a phone, plug it in, then the operator will connect it for you."

"I don't know which room I want it in," Jonnie said.

"It plugs in. You can change it from room to room."

The phone had to be kept in the kitchen because Jonnie's mother would call him every night and disturb their studying.

"Mother, please wait until after nine o'clock to call. We're busy studying until then."

One day there was a large fancy envelope in the mailbox. It was the invitation to the wedding.

"We will have to get them a wedding present," Marty said.

There was a lot of talk over the phone about the wedding.

"Where are you going on your honeymoon?" Jonnie asked his mother.

"Right after the wedding Francis starts his new job. We're moving to Newcastle. It's going to be expensive setting up our new home so we will only have a short honeymoon and spend the rest of the time moving."

"I thought the department would move you."

"Yes, Jonnie, they do, but neither of us have much furniture. We'll have to furnish our home. That's going to be expensive."

"You concentrate on furnishing your home. I'll take care of your honeymoon. Marty is friendly with a local travel agent. I'll find something nice."

"Jonnie, you can't give us a honeymoon."

"Mother, we were saving up to buy a car. We really don't need a car so we'll give you a honeymoon instead. We want to do something special for you two."

"Jonnie, dear, you have always been so good to your mother."

Thursday lunch time Sharon told Jonnie she could roll the board all the way to its end without falling off.

"Great, I'll come by Saturday afternoon and we'll go riding."

"I doubt if I'll be able to do that the first day."

"You stopped me before I could finish. I was going to say, riding up and down the driveway." Sharon laughed. Then Jonnie said, "You appear to be a lot happier than when I saw you last week."

"Jonnie, you're good medicine for me. None of that other crowd taught me anything. All they did was spend money and gossip. You're much more fun."

Jonnie didn't say anything. He smiled and thought, I am fun until some guy comes along in a car.

The bell rang. "See you Saturday, Jonnie."

Jonnie and Marty stopped by to see Mr St Clare, the lawyer. He was glad to see them.

"Have you seen the papers?" he said excitedly.

The boys shrugged their shoulders.

"How about the evening news?"

"We came over here instead of listening to the news."

"I am the most famous lawyer in the country. I got Jonny Rizzoli off. Buy a paper tomorrow morning, the full story will be in it."

"Congratulations," they both said together.

Mr St Clare served them drinks then told them the story.

"It was just like in the movies. The prosecutor objected to me having the ship captain for a witness. I explained to the judge that he was important to the case. When the captain finished his testimony, I stood up and said, in a loud clear voice, 'Your honour, I ask the court to dismiss all the charges against my client. As the witness explained, my client does not deal in illicit drugs. He was there to pick up a shipment of cigarettes.'" Mr St Clare was getting excited as he continued. "The prosecutor went mad. He began screaming at me. The reporters were climbing over each other trying to get to the telephones. It was better than any movie. I'm famous. The whole law society was in the club celebrating all afternoon. I didn't have time to drink. I was shaking hands all afternoon.

"That's great, sir," Jonnie said. "We're happy for you."

"I can never do enough for you boys. Getting mugged was the best thing that happened to me because I met you. Because of you, my life has been turned around. I will be forever grateful."

Saturday afternoon, Marty and Jonnie rode down Sharon's driveway into her backyard. She was tossing baskets so Jonnie jumped off his board and took the ball away from her and sank a basket. They fooled around for a while, trying to outdo each other. When they stopped Jonnie said, "How come you were tossing baskets? You should be practicing on the balancer."

"I can do that in my sleep. I'm ready to roll."

"Let's find out, here's your skateboard."

Jonnie had a board strapped on his back He put it on the ground and gestured for Sharon to stand on it. He had to hold her. He pulled her around then let her go. She didn't fall off.

"I told you I was ready," she said with a smile.

"Don't brag too soon. Come on, it's time for the big test."

They walked to the head of the driveway. It had a little slope, just enough for the board to roll on its own.

Sharon stood on the board and rolled down the drive. She didn't fall off.

"Very good, you have been practicing. Do that for the rest of the afternoon, then we'll go out on the footpath tomorrow."

"I'm ready now, why wait until tomorrow?"

"If you fall you won't get on the board again. Build up your confidence before you try to fly."

After a few more tries, Sharon was brave enough to give herself a little push when she started. She screamed and jumped off the board. "It took off," she said, "it was going too fast."

"That was good. Do it again. I'll be down here to stop you if you go too fast."

After a few times, Jonnie had to admit Sharon was ready to go out on the footpath.

When Sharon screamed, her mother came out to watch. She said to Marty, "Sharon has completely changed since Jonnie was here last week. We were worried about her. She was running with a bad crowd. We were glad when she stopped associating with them, but then she would just mope around. Now she's more like her old self.

"Jonnie would not admit he missed her. You can see they get along well with each other. I wonder if it will last."

"We will just have to wait and see," her mother said. "It's called growing up."

The three of them rode up and down in front of Sharon's house until she was confident.

"That's enough for today, "Jonnie said. "You shouldn't ride around here. You'll attract unwanted attention."

Sharon looked at Jonnie but didn't say anything. She knew he was right.

"Where do you guys practice?" she asked.

"We go to the mall parking lot early in the morning," Marty said. "It's nice and smooth and no one is around."

"Come and get me tomorrow morning. I'll practice with you."

"I thought your family went to church in the morning," Jonnie said.

"Not any more. Someone made a loud rude remark about me so my father complained to the reverend, but he refused to speak to that person. She gave a lot of money to the church so we don't go there any more. Mother and father are disillusioned. They can't understand why the reverend would put money first."

"Seven o'clock," Jonnie said, "see you then."

They rode to the Chinese for a takeaway meal. Back at the clubhouse, Marty asked Jonnie why he didn't stay for supper.

"You used to eat there all the time."

"I'm not going with her any more. We're just friends."

"Her mother said she's a lot happier since you have been coming around."

"Maybe so, but I don't trust her. The first guy with a car and she'll be off."

***

They came on their bikes. Jonnie had a harness for Sharon's board They had a great time riding around the car park. Sharon steadily improved as she gained confidence. When the cars started coming in they rode to the park. They stopped on the way at a small café for a coffee.

"I though you didn't have any money," Sharon said as they sat drinking their coffee.

"We have a steady job now, so I can indulge in the finer things of life."

Sharon giggled. "You always make me laugh."

"An old man told me the best part of his day was when he went to the coffee shop and sat with his friends and talked. He was right, what's better than this? Sitting here with your friends drinking coffee and talking."

Sharon looked at Jonnie then Marty. A tear fell on her cheek and she began to sob. "I'm sorry, Jonnie, I was so wrong about you, and you too, Marty. You are so right. I was never happy or content with the snobs and I have had a better time this morning than all the time I spent up north."

Sharon stood up and walked away. She walked to the corner and stood there for a little while, then returned sat down and finished her coffee. They rode the rest of the way to the park without talking. Marty rode off so they could be alone.

"You must think I'm awful, Jonnie. I have been foolish. I realize I was wrong and will try to make it up to you, if you'll let me."

"Sharon, we're just teenagers. This is part of growing up. We have to go through these things to grow up. Don't be upset and don't feel sorry. You're learning, that's all there is to it. We're too young to be serious with each other. Another boy will come along with a car and you'll go off with him. Later you'll come back and say you're sorry. I can't do anything about that because I'm not normal. I can only do what I can under the conditions I have to live with. You don't have to live under those conditions. Let's leave it at that and be friends without getting serious. And making silly plans we cannot keep."

Sharon did not answer. They were sitting on a bench. She put her head on Jonnie's shoulder and was quiet. They could see Marty doing tricks on his board further along. Finally Sharon said, "Do you think I will ever be able to skate like that?"

"Marty is about the best skater around. You'll be able to do those tricks, but I doubt if you'll ever get more than a five or six."

Sharon sat up and said, "I can play basketball as good as you can so I bet I can skateboard that good too. I may never be as good as Marty, but I can keep up to you. After you teach me, of course."

"You're on. Come on, you're about to get your first lesson."

The spell was broken; Sharon and Jonnie healed the doubt they had about each other.

After skating around the park until noon, Marty left to go to his parents' house for lunch. Sharon said she thought he should go with him.

"I'll stay with you and have lunch at your parents'."

"We're not going anywhere until you tell me what's going on. How come Marty has to be home for Sunday lunch? Has he done something wrong? And why do you have to go with him? I want to know what's going on between you two."

"I'll tell you this afternoon. It's late, we should be at your place now."

"We're not going anywhere until you tell me what's going on."

"All right, but your parents are going to wonder where you are."

"No excuses, start talking." They sat down on the same bench.

Jonnie started by saying, "My mother is getting married. She has met a nice man and they have decided to get married. I'm happy for them."

"What has that got to do with Marty having to have Sunday lunch at home?"

"After the wedding they're moving to Newcastle."

"Jonnie, are you going with them? What's going to happen to us?"

"Her future husband is a policeman. He's being transferred."

"Jonnie, stop it, you're teasing me. Start at the beginning and tell me everything."

"Marty and I have changed our course from general to business. We're studying business because we're going to start our own business after we graduate."

"You told me that last year. I want to know what's going on now."

"My mother is moving away, but I'm not going with her. I'm staying here with Marty to finish high school. I can't live at Marty's house so Marty and I moved into the clubhouse. We have been living there since before school started. Marty's parents allowed him to move in with me on condition that he had Sunday dinner with them so they could keep track of him. I was going too until you came into the picture."

Sharon stared at Jonnie. She could hardly believe what he was saying. Finally she spoke. "You are really serious about starting your own business. I thought it was just a dream you had. You amaze me, Jonnie."

"Sharon, look at me. I could never get a good job in the real world. Marty would have a hard time too. We have a goal and so far we have stuck to it. Just like some kid dreaming to be a fireman or an astronaut. It's the only chance we have to have a good life. We have to succeed. It took a lot of guts to change courses. We were breezing through school before. We're struggling now to keep up with the class. We have to succeed otherwise we will never get anywhere. This is why we're so busy. We have to study and we have to work to pay our expenses. So far we're ahead. Having a girlfriend will complicate things and bust our budget."

"We'll work something out. You came snooping around and got me interested in you again. I'm staying. You're not going to get rid of me."

"Do you really mean that, Sharon? I was devastated when you went away, then you took up with that other crowd when you returned. Are you really going to be my girlfriend or are we just going to be friends?"

Sharon held Jonnie's head and kissed him. "I said I was sorry and I meant it. I have had more fun this morning than all the time I have been away. I know where I belong."

They sat with their arms around each other. Sharon had her head on Jonnie's shoulder. Finally Sharon stood up and took Jonnie's hand. "Come on, we're going to my place for lunch."

"Where are your parents?" Jonnie asked when they went into the house.

"They're in the city for the day."

Sharon took Jonnie's hand and led him into her bedroom. She kissed him then pulled off his shirt..

"Sharon, we can't, I don't have any condoms."

Sharon dropped her slacks then removed her blouse. She reached for her purse and handed Jonnie a condom. "Mother gave them to me when I went up north. I've used two of them."'

Jonnie could not protest. He wanted Sharon. He used to remember the good times every time he saw her at school. They spent the afternoon making up for what they'd missed while they were apart.

Later, Marty found them tossing baskets in the back yard.

"Where have you been? I came by earlier but no one was here."

"We hung around the park until we got hungry," Jonnie said.

"It looks like you've made up," Marty said.

"We're going to be friends," Sharon said, "not serious like we were before."

"We had a long talk," Jonnie said, "and we decided that we have to succeed so Sharon is going to study business with us. We can be serious later."

"That's sensible," Marty said, "but how long is it going to last? I doubt that you will do much studying."

"Jonnie's right," Sharon said, "there isn't much we can do on our own. We have to build up our own business if we want to have anything in this life."

"With you pushing us we will succeed," Jonnie joked.

As Marty and Jonnie were about to leave, Jonnie told Sharon, "We won't see you next Saturday. My mother is getting married. Marty and I are going to Wollongong for the wedding. We won't return until Sunday night."

"We'll have lunch together at school."

***

Jonnie talked with his mother almost every night on the phone. He wanted to do something for her wedding but could not think of anything.

"Where are they going on their honeymoon?" Marty asked.

When Jonnie asked her mother what they had planned for a honeymoon she told them they were not going to have one.

"We're going to come back to Sydney and gather up our belongings then find an apartment in Newcastle. By the time we do that Francis will be starting his new job. We'll have our honeymoon when he has a vacation."

That's what I will do, Jonnie thought, I will shout them a honeymoon.

He spent an afternoon in a travel agency. The proprietor was a friend of Harold Wilson so Jonnie got a ten day ocean cruse for two for five hundred dollars.

He told his mother not to make any plans because he and Marty had been saving up so they could have a honeymoon.

"We'll pack your things while you're away and Mr Wilson will move them to Newcastle. "

"That's wonderful, Jonnie, we really appreciate that."

"I want you to be happy, Mom, you deserve it."

The only time either Marty or Jonnie had ever ridden on a train was with their parents when they were young.

"We'll stay close to each other and not talk to anyone," Jonnie said as they entered the station to ride to central to get the Wollongong train.

They had never been to Central Station. They stood in the concourse reading all the timetables. There were crowds of people moving around them. They were relieved that they did not have to wait long for their train.

Jonnie soon realized that adults did not harass them. Some looked at them but only school children made rude remarks or called them names. They had a pleasant journey—there were no school children on the train.

The journey gave Jonnie an idea. He and Sharon would dress as adults when they went out. We can go on dates; the kids will leave us alone, he thought.

Francis and Ida met them at the station. They had a tour of the city then were taken out for dinner. They stayed with the adults at their apartment. The next morning was the wedding.

It was a casual affair at the city clerk's office. Jonnie gave his mother to Francis and friends from the police were the witnesses. They all had lunch at a fancy restaurant. Jonnie gave them the cruise tickets. They were pleased and surprised.

"These tickets cost you a lot of money," his mother said. "We can't accept them."

"You have to, Mom. They were sold to us by a friend at cost price. We can't get a refund. Marty and I saved up for them so you could have a nice honeymoon."

Francis thanked them and shook their hands.

They had an enjoyable time then left for home.

Jonnie was confused. He'd thought there would be a party that evening, then they would leave the next day for home.

"We'll stay in a motel tonight," Francis said, "then go on the cruise tomorrow. You planed this perfectly, Jonnie. I start my new job in two weeks. We will be back in time to make the move to Newcastle."

Ida and Francis had vacated their apartments when they moved to Wollongong. All their possessions were stored at the clubhouse. All Jonnie had to do was ship them to their new apartment when they found one.

It was late in the afternoon when they arrived home because they drove along the ocean road and stopped for coffee. Marty convinced Jonnie to spend Sunday studying instead of spending it with Sharon. "We're way behind in our studies."

CHAPTER FOURTEEN

Marty and Jonnie resumed their regular routine and it went well for a couple of weeks, until Sharon started coming to the clubhouse after school. She said she wanted to study with them but before long she and Jonnie would retire to Jonnie's bedroom.

This caused them to struggle with their studies and made things difficult between Marty and Jonnie.

"You'll have to tell Sharon not to come here after school," Marty told Jonnie when they got a low mark on an assignment. "We're falling behind in our studies."

"You can say that because you don't have a girlfriend. If Gloria was here you would be doing the same thing."

"Jonnie, you have all your life to be with Sharon. We only have this year to begin our careers. If we fail now we will be bums instead of successful businessmen. Is it worth it to throw all that away for a little sex right now? Get control of yourself. Sharon will not hang around with a bum. You have to give her a good life."

Jonnie did not answer. He went for a long walk in the cold night air. He realized Marty was right. They had put all their time and energy into becoming successful and he was about to destroy all their hard work.

I'll talk with Sharon and hope she will understand, he told himself.

That Sunday afternoon Jonnie and Sharon rode to the park instead of going to the clubhouse. He was building up courage to talk to Sharon.

"Sharon, dear, we're falling behind in our schoolwork. If we don't graduate with a good mark we cannot go to a business college. If we do not have a business degree there are only a few businesses we can operate. I want to give you a good life, but we can't do that if we don't graduate with good marks."

"You're trying to tell me not to visit you at the clubhouse, right?"

"Sharon, you have to understand, we have put a lot of effort into becoming successful. We cannot throw it all away now. Not only that, we'll be dragging Marty down with us. I want us to be successful and have a good life together. We will not have anything if we have to work for someone."

Sharon was quiet for a while then she said, "I was disappointed too with the results of our last assignment. I know we have to struggle to get ahead, but I love you, Jonnie, and want to be with you."

They sat on the bench not talking until Sharon said, "I'm only doing this because I love you. I'll stay away from the clubhouse during the week but I will be there when you finish work on Saturday and stay with you all weekend. Marty will have to find something to do on his own."

"What will your parents say about that?"

"My mother already knows we're sleeping together. I will explain the facts to her. She told me her and father lived together for a long time before they told anyone about it so she cannot condemn me for doing the same. I want us to have a good life, Jonnie, and I'm willing to do anything to make it happen."

"Thank you, Sharon, dear, I did not know what I would have done if you had not understood."

"You would have had to choose between Marty and me."

"I could never do that, it's too awful to even think about."

***

Jonnie's mother returned from the cruse then they moved to Newcastle. Jonnie and Marty settled back into a routine and their marks improved. Marty did not want to be alone on the weekend so he would stay with Mr Wilson on Saturday afternoon and spend Sunday with his parents. Things were running along smoothly until one Monday morning when Gloria appeared in their home room.

They were not able to speak to her until after school. They all met and walked to Gloria's new house together. She had a lot to tell them so they spent the afternoon with her.

"It was a big mistake moving to Tasmania. My father has a good job with his brother and my mother enjoys being with her family, but it was a disaster for me. The school is way behind us here. They were doing first year work in the third year. I was not learning anything."

"What about your dancing career?" Marty asked.

"That was the same. The dance school was a joke. I knew more than the instructor. Also, she did not have any connections with any theatre company. I realized that I could never be a dancer because the boys would not partner with me because I was so small. The same thing would happen on the stage. I would only be able to do children's roles and how many of them are there? I came back here to finish high school. I'm living with my mother's sister and her husband. Their children have left home so I was welcome. I would have never got anywhere staying in Tasmania."

"What are you going to do when you graduate?" Sharon asked.

"I don't know. I do know dancing is out of the question. Marty wanted me to do a business course so I could help him but I doubt if he wants me around after I walked out on him."

"I walked out on Jonnie, too, Sharon said, "but I realized I made a big mistake and he forgave me. Maybe Marty will forgive you and we can be friends again."

"What do you think about that, Marty?" Jonnie asked. "The gang will be together again."

Marty was quiet during the conversation. He had been upset ever since he saw Gloria earlier.

"This is a big shock, I will have to think about it. Welcome back, Gloria. I will not object to you joining the group again but I will have to think about you and me."

"Thank you, Marty. I understand. We can talk about it later."

That put a cloud over the group and Jonnie and Marty left soon after so Sharon and Gloria could catch up.

On the way to the clubhouse Marty said, "I don't want to talk about it right now. I have a lot of thinking to do."

When Sharon saw Jonnie at lunch on Thursday she asked him to keep Marty at the clubhouse on Saturday. She was going to bring Gloria along so she could talk with him.

"I will have to tell him. I don't know what he is thinking because he has not talked about her."

"I hope they can get back together," Sharon said, "then it will be like it was before. We had some good times together."

Marty realized that he had to face the situation sometime so he reluctantly agreed.

Everyone was at their best when the girls arrived. Gloria was shy. She walked around the room and said,

"The place has changed since I was here last. Where is the trampoline?"

"We don't have time to practice," Jonnie said, "so we sold the trampoline and all the gym equipment."

"What did you do that for? It was the best equipped gym around. You could have used it on the weekends."

"We decided that if we didn't practice regularly we could hurt ourselves," Marty said, "so we decided to move on with our lives. We're going to be successful businessmen. We don't have time to fool around any more. It's hard enough keeping up with our schoolwork."

The others were stunned because Marty was so abrupt. He walked into the other room after he spoke. After a moment Gloria followed him.

"I'm sorry, Marty. I know I have hurt you. I had big dreams like you have but mine did not come true. We all have to follow our dreams."

"Gloria, you have a right to your dreams and you pursued them no matter what the cost. I am sorry they did not include me. I have my dream too and I am determined to follow it. I am sorry you did not want to be part of it."

They were standing in the entrance looking at each other.

"Come for a walk," Gloria said, "we have a lot to talk about."

They walked for a bit then Marty said, "There isn't anything to talk about. You dropped me and ran away, that's all there is to it."

"I thought a lot about you."

"You said you would write but you never did."

"Marty, I soon realized that I had made a big mistake but I had to go with my parents. It took me a long time to convince them to let me return. Then more convincing to have my aunt and uncle take me in. I wanted to come back here to you. I really did not want to leave so I had to convince myself that I could be successful on my own."

"Gloria, it hurt when you left and it took me a long time to get over you. I have a routine and a goal now and am struggling to achieve it. I can barely keep up with the lessons. It is a lot harder than the general course. I do not have any spare time and I cannot be distracted. When Jonnie took up with Sharon it upset everything and all our marks went down. We had to agree on a strict routine to keep up with our schoolwork. The same thing will happen again if we start seeing each other. I cannot afford another low mark, it will bring my average down. I need that average to qualify for a business course. Besides, how do you know you will not take off again on another dream?"

They walked around the block not speaking until they came back to the entrance and Marty said, "I am not going back inside with you because we will end up in bed."

"Then walk me home. I want to talk some more."

They walked for a bit then Gloria spoke. "Sharon told me of her time with the socialites at school and what a mistake she made. She realized that she would never find another man as good as Jonnie and was glad when he came around to talk to her. Marty, I have realized the same thing. I was appalled at the conditions in Tasmania. They live good but they are way behind us and there is no future there for young energetic people like us. I missed you all the time I was there and was ashamed to write and say so. I thought I was trapped there until I thought of the school thing. It took a lot of convincing to get my parents to let me return. One of the conditions is that I am to stay away from you. They like you but are convinced you are going to get me to join a circus group with you. They do not want me to join a circus. If my aunt sees me with you she will tell my parents and they will take me back to Tasmania."

Marty had to laugh. "Where did they get that circus idea?"

"You were always doing tricks on your bike and skateboard and we were practicing on the trampoline. Why did you sell it? I liked bouncing on it."

"Jonnie and I realized we could not practice so we decided we could make a mistake and hurt ourselves. Jonnie would not recover from a broken bone. Our overall goal is more important."

"Marty, I understand your struggle. I will not interfere with your routine, in fact I can help. The business course is easy for me. I can help you study on weekends. We can see each other and slowly heal our hurts. I miss you, Marty, and realize, like Sharon, I would be foolish to leave you again. Marty, dear, I will do everything I can to help you so we can have a successful business and a good life together. Now kiss me and say you forgive me."

Marty was startled by what Gloria said. She was right. He missed he and wanted to forgive her. They kissed and they both had a tear in their eyes.

When they were near Gloria's aunt's home she said, "Sharon will pick me up in the morning and we can be together all day. I will tell my aunt I am going to her house to help her study."

Marty was confused but happy as he walked home. He told his mother he would have supper with them that night because he and Jonnie were going to clean up their apartment tomorrow.

Marty had a hard time concentrating. As soon as Gloria arrived his desire for her was almost too strong for him to control. He knew he had to be strong. If he gave in now all would be lost. He soon realized that Gloria was right. The course was easy for her. She stood at the whiteboard like a teacher and with some hard concentration he was soon engrossed in the lesson.

They studied until lunch. It was hard because they had to solve a problem and write their reasons for solving it. It was easy to solve but they had to figure out four different reasons.

They discussed other lessons over lunch then Jonny put the dishes in the sink. He nodded to Sharon and she walked into the bedroom with him. Gloria looked at Marty. He jumped up and took her hand. They had a lot of making up to do.

The gang settled into a routine of school, studying and working. Their grades improved and before long it was the last week of school before exams.

"We're going to study all the time until exams are over," Jonny said. "We can do it for two weeks."

"Then we will celebrate," Marty added.

They all knew this was what they had struggled for so they spent every day reviewing the whole course.

Now that he and Gloria were together again, Marty became his old happy self. He'd missed Gloria and now he had a goal, to have a happy successful life. But one thing nagged him. He did not like sneaking around to avoid Gloria's relatives, so one evening when he was walking her home he spoke to her about it.

"My love, one day we are going to have to tell your parents. I do not like hiding in the shadows to avoid your uncle and aunt."

"I know, dear, I want to tell them too but I do not know how to do it. I am afraid they will take me back to Tasmania if I say anything."

"Gloria, they cannot make you go with them. We are nearly adults, there isn't anything they can do."

"I know, but I do not want to cause my parents to disown me. I love them too much."

"You love me too. I have written a letter to them explaining what we are doing. I want you to put it in your next letter. It will help to break the ice."

"What if they do not understand?"

"We have to do it now because they will be here for your graduation. The letter will ease the shock."

"All right, I will do it. We have to tell them sometimes. I will stay with you, Marty, but it will hurt to go against my parents.'

"I am sure they will understand, they were young too. I bet they went through the same thing."

"Maybe they did. Mother told me it took a long time before father's parents would accept her. When I arrived my mother was accepted because she produced a grandchild.."

"Gloria, I know your parents want you to be happy. Tell them we love each other and want to spend our lives together. They will understand."

***

It was the last week of school and everything was running smoothly until Marty and Jonnie came in after school and found a letter stuffed under the back door. It was an official looking letter.

"I do not like this," Marty said. "That letter looks official."

"It's from our landlord," Jonnie said. "He probably wants to increase out rent."

167

The letter read: 'Young gentlemen, I would like to thank you for looking after the property and keeping it in good condition. Because of its good condition and the location, I have been able to raise the funds to erect a block of flats on the site. You have a month to vacate the premises so demolition can begin. Because you have been good tenants consider your rent paid.' There was a legal paper and a drawing of a three-storey block of flats with the letter.

"This is awful," Jonny exclaimed. "We have to study for exams. We can't spend any time cleaning out this place."

"Relax, Jonnie, Mr Wilson will clean out most of it. We will have to find a new place to live, that's all."

"You have forgotten about the herd of elephants?"

"What are you talking about, what elephants?"

"The ones living in the basement. We have to take them with us."

"You're playing games with me. There isn't anything in the basement except…"

Marty stopped in mid-sentence and shouted, "Holy shit, the armoured car. What are we going to do? The room is full of furniture and boxes."

"Calm down, Marty, I'll talk to my uncle. He can tell the landlord that we are in the middle of exams and need more time. But that is not our biggest problem. We have to dispose of the truck and get all that money out too."

"I forgot about that. If they find the truck that will be the end of our perfect crime. I know, we will cut it up and dump the pieces."

"We could dispose of the body that way but what about the motor and the other heavy pieces? We figured everything else out. We will solve this problem too."

"I suppose we will but we have to do it now. I know, we will repaint it and sell it. Maybe Mr Wilson will buy it."

"You did it again, Marty, you are brilliant."

"Really, what did I do?"

"We sand off the security sign and paint a bakery sign then park it in the bakery parking lot. They will never know the difference."

The boys whooped and hollered and jumped around. Then Jonnie said, "Come on, let's go check out the bakery."

They rode around the bakery parking lot doing tricks and looking over the trucks.

"Most of these trucks came from the security company," Marty said. "They will never notice another one."

"Some of them have a stick on sign on them," Jonnie added. "We have it made."

They returned to the clubhouse and spent the afternoon sanding the security names off the van.

That evening Jonnie and Marty had supper with Jonnie's Uncle Freddie. They showed him the notice to vacate.

"I met the landlord yesterday," Freddie said. "He told me the council would not approve his plans. He has to redesign the building and resubmit the plans. That will take two or three months. Maybe longer, because he is short of funds, but I would be looking for a new place to live."

"That is a relief, "Jonnie said. "We have exams and graduation coming up. We had planned to stay there until after we finished tech college but now we will have to find somewhere to live."

"Don't worry, you have all summer. You will find something."

"I am sure we will but it will cost us a lot of money. We did not plan on something like this happening."

"You have learned a valuable lesson," Freddie said. "Never stretch yourself to the limit. Always have a little kitty for emergencies."

The next morning their teacher surprised them with a trip to the stock exchange.

"The exchange takes new cadets every year. Most of the time they are recommended by members but this year they will show you around and if you like it you will spend the summer as a cadet. Then some of you will be asked to join one of the companies as a trainee. This is a rare opportunity I want you to think about it and only those who are interested should take the tour. Jonathon Eastwood, I know you are interested. Are there any others?"

Two other students put their hands up.

"Marty put your hand up," Jonnie exclaimed, "this is a great opportunity."

"I'm not interested in the stock market. I will stay here with the girls."

"The rest of the class will tour Grace Brothers Department Store in the city. You will travel on a bus and have lunch in the cafeteria."

Some kids dreamt of being firemen or policemen and were excited when they visited a fire or police station. Jonnie was excited when he stood at the rail in the mezzanine and watched the turmoil below. The two other students were frightened by the noise and confusion but Jonnie was fascinated. He intently watched what was happening. He had read the book Mr Wilson gave him and anything else he could find on the stock exchange. He soon sorted out the confusion. The buyers sitting in their booths could not see the board because of the crowded floor so their clerks read the board and signalled them with hand signals. Each company had its own signals so no one else could read them.

To a stranger it was noise and confusion with a crowd of people moving around the floor waving their hands in the air, but Jonnie soon understood what was going on.

The teacher took them down on to the floor. She told them to stay out of the way and if they got lost to meet at the main entrance at noon.

Jonnie could not stand in the back; he was soon in the middle of the vortex. He did not have to go to the front to see the board—he was a head taller than everyone there. He slowly walked along behind the crowd and took in everything that was happening. He soon figured out the routine. He wrote down a few figures of the stocks he was following in the newspaper. He quickly realized that the paper was a day behind what was actually happening. He realized he had to be here on the floor if he wanted to make any real money.

One of the clerks saw a student on the floor. He came over to tell him to return to the rear of the room. When he saw Jonnie writing in a note book he spoke to him.

"Hello, son, do you understand what's going on down here?"

"Yes, sir, I have been reading about the workings of the exchange. I am also following Robert Strange in the newspaper.

"That is interesting. What have you learned today?"

"I picked out a few stocks to follow in the paper. I soon realized the paper is a day behind. One of the stocks is moving. I could have made some money if I had bought it yesterday."

"You can follow the stock movement?"

"About three months ago I began following Mr Strange. I picked out a few stocks to play. I am way ahead of Mr Strange and one of my stocks is moving.

Someone is buying them up a block at the time. They must know something."

"You are ahead of Bobby Strange, that is interesting. Come with me, I would like you to meet my boss. By the way, I am Charlie Green, who are you?"

"I am Jonathon Eastwood. I am here with my high school class."

"Charlie why aren't you out on the floor?"

"It's quiet right now. I have someone I want you to meet. He is a fan of yours."

"He is one of the students getting in the way Why should I meet him?"

"Boss, this is Jonathon Eastwood. He is following Bobby Strange in the paper."

"So what, a lot of people follow him."

"Jonnie started three months ago. He caught up to Bobby in a month and is way ahead of him now."

"Come on, Charlie, he is telling you stories."

"Son, show the boss your figures."

Jonnie handed his notebook to the boss.

"Well, well, you are the clever one."

"I started with a hundred dollars," Jonnie said, "imaginary money. I do not have any money to play with and besides, no broker would talk to me. I am now way ahead of Mr Strange."

"I can see that. It's just good guessing. No one is smarter than Bobby Strange."

"Show the boss your figures on Acme Industries," Charlie said.

"Sir, I have been following Acme as one of my preferred stocks. It is on the move."

"Acme has not moved for years. Most people keep it because it gives a good dividend."

"It has climbed fifty-two cents since I have been here. Look at my figures."

"You are right. Charlie, get out there and check on Acme."

"He does not have to, give me those glasses, I can see it from here."

Jonnie took the glasses and read the figures off the board.

"It has climbed another five cents," the boss said. "Something is going on."

The boss picked up the phone. "Harry check on Acme Industries… What, someone is quietly buying it up. Who?"

"You are on to something, son. I think I know who is doing this. What, Sammy Gold. Harry, buy all the Acme you can at one, two three."

"Harry is our agent," Charlie said. "Buying one, two, three means, buy one block at the time."

"If Sammy Gold is buying that means they are about to dump a bundle on the floor. No one outsmarts me. We are going to make a killing. Son, read me the latest figures."

"I cannot, sir, the numbers keep changing. They are going up all the time."

"Wonderful. Tell me when they stop."

"The Acme line is blinking, sir."

Just then there was a shout from the crowd on the floor. They all started shouting and signalling to the desks. It was like a whirlwind on the floor. The boss just sat there and smiled. Jonnie was fascinated, watching the proceedings. After about ten minutes he said to the boss, "Sir, the board has stopped."

"Quick, read the numbers to me."

Jonnie read the numbers across the board. He was told to keep reading them until they stopped.

Jonnie did not know how long he read the numbers. Then they stopped. The boss picked up the phone and said, "Harry sell Acme one, two, three. Yes, I said sell, I do not care how much it is worth. Sell now."

He put the phone down and said to Jonnie, "Son you are a wonder. We just made a whopping five thousand dollars."

"That is great, sir, but why are you selling?"

"I know what I am doing. Acme is a small company. It just increased by three million dollars. That is about three times its worth. Read the board."

"The price has dropped by five cents."

"It will drop back to close to where it started. Sammy Gold will be investigated but they will not find anything wrong and we made five thousand dollars. The Stranger wins again."

"I do not understand at all."

"Jonnie, meet Peter Harvey, better known as Robert Stranger."

"I like you, son. You are here to sign up as a cadet, right?"

"Yes, sir, I want to have my own brokerage one day."

"Charlie, get the forms from the desk and sign him up as a trainee before someone else spies him. Welcome to the company, son."

"I do not understand, sir."

"You want to be a stockbroker, right?"

"Yes, I do."

"Well, this is the best place to start, with the biggest company and the smartest brokers. You can start on Monday, be here at ten."

"But, sir, I have exams and graduation. I cannot possibly start before the first of the month."

"I forgot about that. I know, you continue to follow the market at home and phone in your tips every day around noon until you finish school, then come here and learn all about the market."

"Thank you, sir, but the paper is a day behind. I will be wasting your time."

Mr Harvey thought for a minute then said, "You can follow the market on your television, that is up to the minute."

"The news only gives the daily total. How is that going to help?'

"Buy yourself a new television. Make sure it has a Teletext programme. There are pages of market reports on it. You have earned a percentage for your buying

176

today. I will set up a portfolio for you so you can play the market with real money."

"Wow, thank you, sir, I would like that."

"Continue to read the market just like you were doing it before. Do not take wild chances trying to get rich, it does not work. Charlie will explain how to work the system. Don't forget to call in every day and don't get too cocky. You cannot beat me any more because I will be watching your daily report."

"Thank you, sir. I have been studying hard at school so I could go to business college next year. This is a big advancement for me."

"Jonathon you are going to be as good as me in a couple of years."

"Where have you been Jonathon?" his teacher asked. "I was ready to send the ushers to look for you."

"I am sorry, miss. Look, I have been signed up as a trainee. I start after graduation."

"That is wonderful, Jonathon, I am proud of you.'

***

Marty had never been in a large department store. He was looking around as they were ushered along to a meeting room in the rear. After an introductory talk by the manager, different employees spoke of how they liked working here. Then the manager told them how they could put in an application for a job.

"We're being recruited to be shop assistants," Sharon said. "I want to learn how the company works, not work for the company."

"We will not fill out the forms," Marty said. "Look around and learn all you can."

While they were having lunch in the cafeteria, the manager walked among them trying to encourage them to join the company. When he stopped at their table Sharon said to him, "How do you keep track of all the goods that come through here? It must be a difficult job."

The manager smiled and said, "I see that you are more interested in the managerial side of the company. Come with me. I will give you a tour of the purchasing department. We are soon going to expand the floor space so the department is going to move to another building. They do not have to be in the store."

They walked along a long corridor then through a large warehouse and into an office complex.

"This is the distribution department," the manager said. "The goods are sent from our warehouses to all our stores. Upstairs are the buyers. Here we are. There are two different types of buyers. The most experienced ones take our fashion designs and find a manufacturer to make them for us. They have to know quality, material and pricing. The other buyers tour the different manufacturers and choose what suits our customers from their samples."

"That is interesting," Sharon said. "I would like to travel around buying for the company.'

"I like designing," Gloria said. "Because I am small I design my clothes and mother sews them for me. I designed this outfit."

"Really," the manager said. "It looks like an ordinary school uniform to me."

"It is made to suit me. There are two hidden pockets in the pleat of the skirt and the waist band is wide elastic for comfort."

"You are very clever. I like the hidden pockets. May I show it to our seamstress?"

He called a woman who looked at the skirt and said, "You are a very clever young lady. There is a demand for pockets in skirts but I could never hide them well enough. You have solved the problem. May I look at how you did this?"

They went into a changing room so the seamstress could closely examine the sewing.

The manager said to Marty, "What part of this organization do you like?"

"I like selling, sir. I am thinking of going into real estate. I help out in a local agent's office."

"You may be surprised but our shoe salesmen make the most money. They get a bonus for exceeding their quota. Maybe you should look into it."

"I never thought of that, sir, thank you."

The seamstress and Gloria returned.

"This young lady is very clever. I have given her my address here so she can send me some of her designs."

"Will she be paid for them if you use them?" Sharon asked.

The seamstress was surprised by the question.

"Of course. We have many designers who send us their designs. We pay them if we use them."

"That is good to know," Sharon said.

On the way home Gloria said, "I never thought of being a clothes designer. I did it as a hobby. I always wanted to be a dancer. I could have a new career."

"The manager wanted me to sell shoes," Marty said. "I suppose if all else fails Gloria and I can work for Grace Brothers."

They laughed.

Jonnie was waiting for them. He excitedly told him about his good fortune.

"Gloria and I are going to work for Grace brothers," Marty said.

Jonnie did not like that.

That evening Marty and Jonnie visited Martin St Clare.

"You are very fortunate, Jonnie. It is very difficult to get a position on the floor of the market and almost impossible to get a portfolio. I know of one person who had to deposit ten thousand dollars for a portfolio."

"I am going to work my portfolio from home until I graduate. I have to buy a new television with a Teletext on it. Then I start next month at the stock market."

"Well, that takes care of you. What are you going to do, Marty?'

"I am not going to sell shoes, that's for sure. I will carry on and go to business college. By then Jonnie will be able to work from our office. I still want to be a real estate agent."

"I am proud of you two. If all the young people had your enthusiasm we would be the best country in the world."

"We are the best country in the world," Jonnie said.

The next afternoon Marty and Jonnie were working with Harold Wilson. When they took a break Jonnie showed him the eviction notice.

"I have been expecting something. I was going to ask you what you were going to do this summer. I need you guys. I cannot do this work alone. We will get some Chinese and talk about it tonight."

They finished work and stopped for a takeaway. After a nice meal they sat in the lounge and talked.

"Mr Wilson, we do not want you to quit work and move away," Jonnie said. "There must be something we can do to help you."

"I know that I will have some spare time," Marty said. "I can help you and Jonnie will be available on weekends."

Harold smiled. "I did not realize that you were so concerned about me. I am touched, but the truth is I am not well enough to do this heavy work any more. I did not like working in the bank so I did not care about myself. I smoked and drank a lot. I realized when my father died that I had to change my ways so I quit banking and smoking and worked outside. It helped but I never fully recovered. The lifting is too much for me, which is why I hired you two. I have made up my mind. A removalist wants to buy my business. I will not get much for it but at least I will get something."

The boys were about to protest but Harold held up his hand.

"I have thought about it and it is the best thing I can do. They are taking over next week. I am now unemployed."

"What about all the goods you have stored in the clubhouse?" Jonnie asked.

"I am going to borrow this fellow's truck on Saturday. We can clean it out in one day."

"We have some trash to remove too."

"We will remove that tomorrow afternoon after we clean out the things here."

"You have figured it all out," Marty said. "What are you going to do next? I hope you are not going to move from here. We will miss you."

"Where are you fellows going after you clean out the clubhouse?'

"We have not had time to think about that. I suppose we will have to rent an apartment."

"What do you think about moving in here? I have been using some of the rooms for storage. We will clean them out then take your trash and mine to the incinerator. Then you boys can move in."

Jonnie and Marty looked at each other.

"That would solve all out problems," Marty said.

"What about our girlfriends?' Jonnie said.

"I had forgotten about them," Marty said. "That is a big problem."

"You can entertain your ladies here, I do not mind. I was young once, you know."

"It is not you we are worried about," Marty said. "I do not think the girls would feel comfortable here. I mean with a stranger."

"They would soon get to know me. I will not bite them. Any friend of yours is welcome here."

"We have plenty of time," Jonnie said. "We have to get through exams first, then we can decide what to do."

"What about you, sir, what are you going to do once you quit working?"

"I have that all planned out, that is if you guys agree. Jonnie, you will be at the stock market and Marty will be at tech college. Did you know you can do tech at night?"

"We thought it was a full time course," Marty said. "We did not know you can do it at night"

"They do both, the night course is for working people who want to improve their skills. I have an idea for Marty. It depends how old you are. When will you be eighteen, Marty?'

"I am eighteen. My birthday was last month."

"Why didn't you tell me? We could have had a party."

"We were busy studying. We will have a double party for your birthday. Why do you want to know if I am eighteen Mr Wilson?"

"Did you know you can get a real estate licence at eighteen?"

"Yes, sir, but I have to graduate from business college first."

"Who told you that? The government is thinking of changing the rules but that will be years away. All you need is a high school diploma and a job with a registered agent."

"What are you scheming now?"

"Marty graduates and he and I go into the real estate business through the back door."

"You will have to explain yourself," Marty said. "What is this back door?"

"I have a bit of money. You get your licence and we buy up old properties and resell them. We do not need an office or a secretary, just a business name. I can get that and you get the licence. We drive around and buy abandoned properties, hang on to them then resell them later on. The city is about to expand and we will expand with it.'

"It is going to be costly to pay the taxes on these properties," Marty said. "That will use up a lot of our money."

"If we buy ten properties, one of them will pay the expenses and the other nine will be profit. We cannot lose. I have a friend who does repairs. He will fix up the good ones and we can rent them until we sell them or just sell them as a good house."

"I like that idea," Marty said. "I do not have to wait, I can be in business right away. With Jonnie making money on the stock market and me in real estate, we will be rich long before we thought we would."

"What about the girls?" Jonnie said. "Where do they fit into this?"

"The girls can go to business college and run the businesses," Marty said. "I will have some spare time. I can start another business. I have been thinking about selling cars. We could do it the same way as the real estate business. All we need is a storage shed to keep the cars in."

"That is a good idea," Harold said. "Buy them at auction then detail them and sell them from the warehouse. You guys are real businessmen."

"We can get Mr St Clare to do the legal work," Jonnie said.

"Wait a minute," Harold said. "What is this about Mr St Clare? Is that Martin St Clare?"

"Yes, sir," Jonnie said, "he is our lawyer."

"I am a lawyer; how do you know Martin?'

"We have helped him a couple of times," Jonnie said. "He advised us to take the business course at school and then go to business college. We even have a registered business with a name."

"You guys are way ahead of me. Martin and I are old friends. I have not seen him for years."

"We did not know you were a lawyer," Jonnie said.

"Martin and I went through law school together. He got all the breaks and I got all the bum cases. My father persuaded me to quit law and go into banking. When Martin went out on his own he asked me to join him but I was already involved at the bank. How is he? I would like to see him again."

"I will call him," Jonnie said. "Maybe he will see us right away."

"Twice in the same week," Martin said," and you came in the front door, it must be important."

"Mr St Clare, we have brought along a friend who wants to meet you."

"You should know better than to do something like that. He may be someone who does not like me."

"I thought everyone liked you, Martin," Harold said. "Give me a hug."

"Harold, I haven't seen you since your father's funeral. What a surprise."

The two friends hugged and patted each other on the back.

"You look better than the last time I saw you," Martin said."

"I have reinvented myself, thanks to these young men. When they told me they knew you I had to meet you."

"Wonderful, it has been too long. Tell me all about yourself."

The men talked while Jonnie made tea and Marty thumbed through a magazine. Finally the talk swung around to the boys.

"I knew Jonnie had a position at the stock exchange," Martin said, "but I did not realize Marty was going for his real estate license."

"I have some money," Harold said. "We are going to buy disused properties and fix them up. The market is about to boom so they will go up in value."

"That is a good idea. I have a little money so I will join you," Martin said. "When the market starts to move it will not stop."

"We will have a meeting after we graduate to plan this," Marty said.

"In the meantime, I will look around for some good properties to buy," Harold added.

"I have a couple in mind," Martin said. "It looks like we are in business."

CHAPTER FIFTEEN

The next morning Marty and Jonnie met the girls at school.

"Sharon and I are going into the city to Grace Brothers," Gloria said. "I am going to take some of my drawings and a couple of my dresses with me. I know they will like them."

"I know they will," Marty said. "Jonnie and I are going to be busy until Sunday, we will see you then."

"We are supposed to study for the finals. When are we going to do that?"

"We will study all day Sunday and Monday. The first exam is on Tuesday. We have learned all we can. I am sure we will get good grades."

Marty gave Gloria two one dollar bills "Just in case you are short," he said, "keep enough for the train fare home."

Marty and Jonnie spent the morning at the clubhouse gathering up all the trash. There were the rest of the worn notes and all the other trash from living there. They piled the boxes near the main door then went looking for Mr Wilson.

There was a large van backed up to the front door of Mr Wilson's house with a ramp on the porch. Two men were carrying furniture from the house.

"You boys are early," Harold said. "Mr Caffrey and his son offered to help. We are nearly finished. I did not realize I had so much stuff."

"You have a lot more at the clubhouse," Jonnie said. "I hope you saved some furniture for our rooms.'

"And some office furniture too," Marty added.

"I have thought of everything, I hope. We will do some house cleaning then you can furnish your rooms.."

Harold introduced the boys to the removalist. With five of them working it did not take long to finish.

"I have known Mr Caffrey for many years," Harold said. "He was going to open a store but now he is going to sell to established stores like I did. We will gather up the trash then stop for yours, then go to the incinerator. We should finish by lunch time."

"We can come back here and clean the rooms," Marty said.

They picked up all the leftover pieces and loaded them on Harold's truck. He backed into the clubhouse to load the boy's boxes.

"I did not realize I had so much stored here," Harold said. "It will take all day to move this."

"Mr Wilson we will be leaving here soon," Jonnie said, "so you can have Mr Caffrey come here to move this stuff."

"We will help," Marty added.

"Thank you, boys I do not mind doing a little work, but working all day is too much for me. Let's get your trash loaded. I am getting hungry,"

***

Sharon and Gloria very seldom went anywhere alone so they were thrilled to be in the city. Gloria's appointment was at one so they wandered around looking in all the shops.

"This is fun," Sharon said. "We will have to do this more often."

They had a light lunch at the store cafeteria. They met the clothing manager right on one. She looked at Gloria's samples then called the seamstress. The two of then spent a lot of time examining the samples then they sat with Gloria and looked through her drawings. Finally the manager said, "Miss Cloutier, we like your work. There is a gap in out teenage wardrobe your designs would help to fill. In fact, we would like to use some of your designs in our fall presentation."

"That is wonderful," Gloria exclaimed. "I am thrilled."

"We think you have talent but you are behind the trends. We want you to work with our design team to produce a full range of fashions for the young teenager. Will you do that?'

"Designing was only a hobby. I designed my own clothes because I could not find anything suitable in my size. I will study the latest fashions and design a wardrobe for teens. In fact I have a few ideas from looking at the clothes here on display."

They made the arrangements for Gloria to start as soon as she graduated then they walked through the clothing section and Gloria described some of her ideas. The ladies were impressed,.

Gloria was excited walking back to the train station. She was telling Sharon some of her ideas. On the train, after Gloria had calmed down, Sharon said, "You have found a job, Jonnie and Marty have jobs, but I have no idea of what to do. We were all going to business school and that is what I thought we would do. What am I going to do? I am all mixed up."

"Don't worry about it right now, we have exams to get through, then we will sit down and decide what to do. We are all in this together so don't worry, things will work themselves out. We have to stick together to survive."

***

Marty vacuumed and Jonnie dusted They cleaned every room in the large house. When they finished they walked through the house deciding how to set it up for them to live there and where to have the office.

"We will have the rear of the house," Jonnie said. "We can come in and out the back door. Mr Wilson can live upstairs. That way the girls will not mind staying here."

When they told Harold their plan he had other ideas. "I do not want to climb the stairs. You young ones live upstairs. I will live in the back downstairs and the front will be the office. We will keep the kitchen and dining room for our meals. There is a doorway that was in the hallway. I took it down. It is in the garage. We will replace it so it separates the office from the rest of the house. I doubt if there will be many people visiting the office but we need a workspace and that will do both."

"I thought it would be a couple of years before we got started," Marty said, "but we will be in business in a couple of weeks. Let's go upstairs and decide which room we want.

"What are we doing up here?" Jonnie asked. "The girls will decide where we will sleep."

"I want to show you something I discovered while I was vacuuming, it is in here."

Marty took Jonnie into the larger bedroom and showed him the closet.

"It is just a closet, so what?"

"Look at this." Marty went into the closet and pushed on the wall. It clicked then opened. There was a storage space behind the door.

"Wow, a secret room. How did you find it?"

"I backed into it while I was cleaning. I thought it would be full of money but there isn't anything in there. We have the perfect place to hide our money."

"You are right, Marty, it is perfect but how are we going to get the money here?'

"We will stuff it into our bedding when we make the last move, unless you can think of anything better."

"All right, keep that in mind. Now let's go, Mr Wilson is waiting for us."

"We have to finish for the day," Jonnie said. "I have to buy a television set. Mr Wilson, will you take us to the television store?"

Jonnie was very business-like as he looked at all the models on display. He asked the salesman about Teletext and was shown how to operate it. Jonnie chose the largest console model and Harold was surprised when he counted out a bundle of small bills and paid cash for the set. But he did not say anything. They took it to the clubhouse and set it up in the lounge. Jonnie was getting excited waiting for Harold to hook up the aerial. Jonnie tuned into the stock market and was soon engrossed, studying the numbers and writing notes on a pad. Marty and Harold went downstairs and looked over the furniture stored there.

"Now that we know the layout of the house we should pick out some of the good pieces from what is here," Harold said.

"We can load some of it right now," Marty replied.

"Not today, I have done enough. What are you doing tomorrow afternoon?"

"Tomorrow is the last day of school. All we do is hand in our books and clean out our lockers."

"We will go through this stuff tomorrow afternoon. Thank you for all your help today."

Marty looked through the furniture and picked out a few things for his room. He was surprised when the girls came in.

"Marty, I have a job at Grace Brothers," Gloria said excitedly. "I start right after graduation. Where is Jonnie? We want to tell him too."

They went upstairs, but Jonnie was talking on the phone.

"I just made a lot of money," Jonnie said. "I have only had the television for a few minutes and I am already making money. I will soon be rich."

Gloria and Sharon looked at each other and Marty said, "Calm down, Jonnie you are not going to be rich, all of us are going to be rich. We are in this together."

Jonnie looked at his friends then sat down. "I am sorry, I got excited at making my first hundred on the market. You are right, Marty, we are in this together, but it was exciting making my first purchase."

"Gloria has something to tell us," Marty said.

"I have a position at Grace Brothers as a fashion designer. I start after graduation."

"That is wonderful, Gloria, I am happy for you. Marty is going into real estate. We all have jobs except Sharon. What are you going to do, dear?'

"We had planned to start business college but now it looks like I will be going there on my own. I do not have any other plans."

"Don't worry, dear, something will turn up. We have a lot to discuss but we have to get through the exams first, then we will have a conference and decide what to do. A lot of things are happening right now. After the exams we will sort everything out."

"You can start right now," Sharon said. "Where did you get the money to buy that expensive television?"

"I just made it on the stock market. Sharon, dear, soon we will not have any money problems. Let's get through the exams first then everything will sort itself out."

"All right, Jonnie, but you had better have a good explanation. Come on, Gloria, it is time to go home."

"You have done it now," Marty said.

"You were pretty hard on Jonnie," Gloria said.

"He was strutting around like a peacock. Besides, he is always saying he is broke but he can spend big on himself. If I do not control him now I never will. Things are going to be different after graduation."

The next morning the gang met at school. Sharon was pleasant to Jonnie. They cleaned out their lockers then went to a nearby café to talk.

"You have us all confused, Jonnie," Sharon said. "Gloria and I want to know what is going on."

"I am sorry, dear, you will understand after the exams. There is too much going on now to explain."

"All you talk about is after the exams. I think that is an excuse. You are keeping something from us and we want to know what it is."

"Sharon, dear, we have a lot to do today and tomorrow. Mr Wilson has sold his business and we have to help him dispose of it. We will give you all day Sunday and Monday to explain everything to you. It is very complicated and there are more people involved than us."

"You are getting me all the more confused. There is only Mr Wilson besides us."

"There is also Mr St Clare, we have to include him."

"Who is Mr St Clare?'

"He is our lawyer. Mr Wilson is our accountant, then there is the registered business and a lot of other things. It will take all day to explain everything. Our company has grown a lot in the past month. We have a new home and office to show you too. Please, Sharon, trust me. Wait until we can tell you the whole story."

"You have a house and an office. When did all this happen?"

"We are going to clean up Mr Wilson's furniture today and take it to our new home. Tomorrow we are going to clean out the furniture in the clubhouse. We are moving out of the clubhouse right after exams. Sharon, dear, we are too busy to do anything else. We want to wait until the house is furnished before we show it to you. It was going to be a surprise."

Sharon could see that Jonnie was getting upset. She put her arm around him and said she was sorry. "I am upset too all of you have jobs but me. I will have to go to tech on my own."

"Sharon, we are all going to tech together. They have night courses. Everything will be smoothed out after exams. Gloria's parents will be here, and mine too, we will be very busy. We have all summer to plan out future."

"I understand, Jonnie, dear. I will be good for now but you had better be telling us the truth. A house, an accountant and a lawyer. That is a lot to take all at once."

"Sharon, we have been planning this for a long time," Marty said. "A lot of things happened all at once, that is all. We are having a hard time understanding it too. We have jumped ahead a couple of years, that's all."

"Come to the clubhouse and meet Mr Wilson and pick out some furniture," Jonnie said. "If we finish early we can spend the rest of the afternoon together."

They were looking through the furniture when Harold arrived. The girls liked him so everyone was happy. Harold told them what was needed and it did not take them long to pick out the best pieces.

"We can move it right away," Harold said.

He backed the truck in and they soon had it loaded.

"Where are you taking this?" Sharon asked.

"It is going to the new house," Marty said.

"We want to go too. "e want to see the new house."

"But we are not going to move there until after graduation," Jonnie said.

"We can help set up the furniture," Gloria said.

The boys could not argue so the girls rode with Harold and the boys followed on their bikes. The girls ran around the rooms while the boys unloaded the furniture.

"This is a palace," Sharon exclaimed. "I love it. I am sorry I was upset, Jonnie. I understand what you were doing now."

"I like it too," Gloria added. "We will be happy here."

Harold showed them around and explained how the rooms would be laid out. The girls moved the furniture around to suit them then they all sat in the lounge with a cup of tea talking about their new life in their new home. Finally Gloria said she wanted to go home and work on her designs.

"I want to look at the market," Jonnie added.

So they broke up.

"We are working all day tomorrow," Jonnie said. "We will see you on Sunday at the clubhouse."

Jonnie went straight to the television and began scanning the market. Marty did not have anything to do so he studied for the exam.

It was late in the afternoon. The market had slowed down. Jonnie scanned the whole board. It was very quiet. Then he saw something happening to an obscure company. He followed it for about a half hour, then he became suspicious so he called it in.

"So you are the whiz kid they are talking about. I am Harry Tate, the odd member of the team. The market has slowed down for the weekend. I am waiting for the American market to open. What did you call for?"

"I have noticed a movement in Cartwright and Partners. I thought I would call it in"

"Never heard of them. Where did you find them?"

Jonnie explained what he had found.

"That is a two dollar company but it gives a good dividend every year. Give me a minute to look it up."

Jonnie sat at the phone then Harry said, "I think you are on to something. Can you come in? I will explain to you how I trace a company."

"I would like that. It will take me about a half hour to get there, but the market will be closed by then."

"Go to the side door and ring the bell. When the guard comes tell him Harry called you in."

Jonnie was excited. He was going to learn about the market and he was going to travel into the city on his own. He took ten dollars in small notes and told Marty he would be late coming back. He hurried to the train station to start his new adventure.

"You have stumbled on to something," Harry said, when Jonnie settled down in the office. "Cartwright is a small investment company. They have been around for a long time. Their stock is worth two dollars fifty. It hasn't changed for years. Someone is making a run on it, just like Acme. You have a knack of finding these things."

Harry showed Jonnie a large book. "This is a catalogue of all the companies on the market. They are in categories according to the amount of stock they are floating. You can see Cartwright is way down in the two dollar companies but it has always paid a dividend so it is worthwhile in a portfolio. It pays better than bank interest."

Jonnie read about the company then thumbed through the catalogue. "I will have to get one of these books so I can keep learn about all these companies."

"We will get you a copy when the latest one comes out next month. Now I will explain what is going on here. These small companies cannot trade during the day when the market is in full swing. No one pays attention to them so they trade after hours. There are a lot of scalpers who troll the board like sharks looking for an easy dollar. Someone has been slowly buying up Cartwright stocks for a while and now he is going to unload them tonight."

"How do you know that?"

"The scalpers will have a whole file of stocks on hand waiting for a chance to unload them. They buy them quietly over a period then unload them when they think the time is right. This scalper is buying up small parcels all at once to get others interested then the price goes up and more buyers think they are going to make some money so they start buying. That is what is happening now. When the scalper thinks the price has peaked and a lot of people are buying he will dump his load and cash in."

"I can see the price has climbed some more," Jonnie said.

"It is time for us to start buying. That will keep the price climbing."

Jonnie watched while Harry bought up every parcel that came up. Harry stopped after he had bought a thousand shares. The price was still climbing.

"Why did you stop?" Jonnie asked.

"The price is climbing over three dollars. If we buy more we will not make any money, only break even."

"I do not understand."

"This is a two dollar company. It cannot pay a dividend on three or more dollars. Soon everyone will realize that and begin selling. I figure it will reach about five dollars. Then we will sell."

They watched the stock until it slowed down.

"It is stopping at four dollars ninety five," Jonnie said.

"Time to start selling."

Every time an offer came up Harry would sell. "I am not putting our stock up, just selling to buyers. That way it will keep climbing."

They watched and sold until all their stock was gone. It had climbed to five dollars thirty cents before it stopped.

"Watch closely," Harry said. "The scalper is about to drop his bundle."

Sure enough, a bundle of two thousand appeared. Some started to buy but the price began to drop very quickly. Soon it had returned to its original value..

"We did it," Harry exclaimed, "we beat the scalper. The scalper paid five thousand for his bundle. I figure he sold for six thousand. We beat him. Good work, Jonnie."

"I do not understand."

"We spent two thousand in about an hour and doubled out money. The scalper spent a week or more and only made a thousand dollars. We beat him, Jonnie. You have learned a lot tonight. You are on your way to being a top broker. Just keep calm and do not get greedy. You are a natural at this. We just made five hundred each. Good work."

"What happens to the rest of the money?"

"It goes in the company bank. We keep a good reserve for emergencies. A couple times a year we divide up the extra. Don't worry, you will get your share. Come on, we will celebrate."

They went around the corner to an all-night café for a coffee.

When Jonnie arrived home he found the television on and Marty curled up on the lounge. He carried him to his bed and tucked him in.

When Marty woke up it took him a few minutes to realize that Jonnie had put him there. The boys had a quiet breakfast then Jonnie said, "We had better get ready for Mr Wilson, he will be here soon.

They were surprised when they went downstairs and found a truck in the bay half full of furniture.

"I thought you guys were going to sleep all day," Harold said.

It did not take long to finish loading the truck. When it left Harold declared, "I am now officially retired. Let's celebrate. I will buy you breakfast."

They sat in a café discussing what they were going to do next.

"We cannot do anything for the next two weeks," Jonnie said. "We have exams and graduation and my parents will be here for the graduation."

"I can apply for my real estate licence," Marty said. "Maybe we can look at some properties because I will not be as busy as Jonnie."

"I will keep my truck until you guys move," Harold said, "then I will get a car so we can all travel together."

Jonnie looked out the window and was surprised to see Sharon and Gloria walking by. He tapped on the window and waved.

"What a surprise, were going to the clubhouse to see you," Sharon said.

"We are finished," Jonnie said. "A big truck came and took everything away."

"That is great," Gloria said, "now we can hang out for the rest of the day."

Harold drove off while the gang walked to the clubhouse.

Gloria and Marty were holding hands and talking along the way.

"I talked to my mother last night," Gloria said. "We talked about your letter. They are relieved that we are not going to run away to the circus."

"Does that mean we can be seen together?'

"It means that we are going to be together from now on. Marty, we are going to live together I am staying with you all weekend and I will move in with you when you move to our new house."

"That is wonderful, dear. When we are settled we will be married."

"If you are proposing to me, Marty, dear, I accept. We will tell my parents when they arrive."

They spent some time doing tricks on their skateboards in the empty bay but soon they made their way upstairs.

Later Marty found Jonnie in the kitchen looking for something to eat.

"Isn't it wonderful," Jonnie said. "The girls are going to be with us all the time."

"Yes, Jonnie it is wonderful, but we cannot live with them until after we move to the new house."

"What do you mean? They are willing to stay with us now. I think it is great."

"I like it too but you are forgetting our pet elephant. We have to find it a new home before we can settle down with the girls."

"I forgot all about that. What are we going to do?"

"What is this about an elephant?" Sharon asked when she came in the room. "Are we going to the zoo?"

"Just a little joke between Marty and me, dear. There isn't anything to eat. We will have to go out for dinner."

"Wonderful, but how can you afford it? You are always broke."

"I am a big time stockbroker now, we can afford to go out once a week from now on."

They walked to the main street and chose the Chinese restaurant. It was a big treat and they enjoyed it.

On the way back Sharon was walking arm in arm with Jonnie. "I have had a wonderful time, Jonnie, dear. I like our new life. I hope it will always be like this."

The next morning they rode their skateboards to the park then came back to study. The girls went shopping in the afternoon for food and cooked the guys a nice meal.

While they were gone Jonnie said, "Having the girls around all the time is costing us a lot of money.

205

You are going to have to go to work, Marty, to pay your share."

Monday afternoon the girls went off to get some clean clothes so Marty and Jonnie rushed downstairs to the truck.

"We will give it a quick paint job," Jonnie said, "then the next chance we have we will put the signs on it."

It did not take long to paint over where they had sanded out the security company's name. When they finished Jonnie said, "It has been sitting for a long time. I wonder if it will start."

"It better, we are dead if it doesn't."

It would not start; the battery was flat.

"We have had it now," Marty said. "We cannot tow it out of here."

"Don't give up yet. We will go to the garage and buy a new battery. I will say my uncle sent me. Come on, we have to get back here before the girls come back."

It was a heavy truck battery, but it had handles so they carried it between them.

"That was hard work," Jonnie complained. "Let's quit for now."

"We cannot quit, we have to finish this before the girls come back."

They put the new battery in the truck. It started right away. The boys jumped around, glad that they had solved another problem.

When they went upstairs Marty said, "I can smell exhaust fumes. If I can smell them the girls will too. What are we going to do?"

"Open the big door to let the fumes out," Jonnie said. Marty looked out the door and saw the girls coming down the street.

"They are here, we are sprung."

Jonnie gave Marty a broom. "Quick, we are sweeping out the bay."

"We have bought something nice for our dinner," Sharon said. "We are going to cook you a nice meal."

"We will be up when we finish cleaning up," Jonnie answered.

***

The first exam on Tuesday morning was English. It was easy for Sharon but the others struggled. Sharon waited for the others then they walked back together. They spent the day and evening studying for the math test which was next.

The first week they all had the same tests which were standard throughout the state. The next week was their business tests then the different individual elective subjects.

The third week was the minor courses then graduation on the Friday. Thursday was practice day. The gang did not have any minor courses so they prepared for their parents' arrival.

Sharon went home to her parents. Gloria would stay with her aunt while her parents were there. Marty went home too. That left Jonnie alone at the clubhouse. His mother and Francis would stay there over the weekend.

"We have a couple of free days," Jonnie said, "so we can get rid of the elephant."

"What is the hurry? We can stay at the clubhouse until the council approves the new plans."

"You are not thinking. My mother is going to stay there over the weekend. What if Francis gets curious and decides to explore the basement? Besides, the girls want to move into the new house right away. This is our only chance so we have to take it."

"All right," Marty said, "we will lock up the clubhouse in case the girls come by and work nonstop until the truck is gone."

It was easier than they thought it would be. Jonnie had made stick-on signs when they stole the truck so they carefully fitted them on.

While they were working they heard someone knock on the back door and call their names. They were quiet and did not respond then continued working when it was quiet.

"It looks just like their other trucks," Marty said. "We will move it right away."

"We will ride around the parking lot and check it out first," Jonnie said.

The bakery took up one corner of the municipal parking lot. Their trucks had a reserved section in front of their building. Their trucks were coming and going all the time. The boys had checked out the routine before. The trucks were gone for most of the day and returned late in the afternoon. But the bakers worked a different shift. The day shift came in about four in the afternoon to bake the bread for the next day. They left around ten at night then the night shift came in about one in the morning to bake the cakes and things for that day. It was quiet around midnight so that was when the boys would dump the truck.

Marty and Jonnie rode around the parking lot at about ten to look around. The trucks were parked in a row and no one was around.

"Let's go," Marty said, "it's now or never."

They went back to the clubhouse. Marty started the compressor then helped Jonnie remove the heavy planks covering the hole.

Jonnie started the truck and backed it on to the hoist. He sat in it while it was going up.

About three quarters up the hoist stopped. The compressor was making a lot of noise but it was not lifting.

"What is wrong?" Jonnie shouted. "Don't stop now."

"The truck is too heavy the hoist will not lift it," Marty shouted.

Jonnie had just enough room to open the door and jumped out. He put the safety pole down and turned off the hoist.

"Let the compressor build up more pressure then try again. I will be ready to drive it off as soon as it is at the top."

It seemed to take forever before the compressor turned off when the pressure had built up. Jonnie started the truck then told Marty to turn on the hoist.

The truck slowly rose up, then the compressor started, then the hoist stopped a couple of inches before it was level.

"Go, go," Marty shouted. "Jump the curb."

Jonnie revved the motor. The wheels were spinning, the truck's front end jumped up and the hoist shook violently.

The truck jumped out on to the floor and sped across the room. It stopped it just before it hit the overhead door. Jonnie was shaking and covered in sweat.

Marty turned off the compressor then let the hoist down. He ran upstairs to find Jonnie sitting in the truck staring at the overhead door.

"We did it," Marty exclaimed. "Good work, Jonnie. Are you all right?"

"I cannot do this any more. When we deliver this truck I will never do another dishonest thing in my life." Jonnie jumped out of the truck and was walking in circles. "My whole life flashed by. I thought I was going to crash through the door. This is crazy."

It took Jonnie some time to calm down. He was sitting on the floor next to the overhead door. Finally he got up and said, "Come on, let's get this over with before I chicken out."

Jonnie started the truck while Marty opened the door. He closed it then jumped in the truck.

"Don't forget to turn on the lights," Marty said. "We do not want the cops to stop us."

"That is all we need. That would put paid to all our plans."

Jonnie carefully drove to the bakery. He parked the truck between the others. They jumped on their skateboards and rode into the night.

Jonnie was pumped full of adrenaline. He rode around the back streets for about a half hour before he calmed down.

"I am hungry," he said. "Let's get a pizza."

There was no one in the shop so they sat and ate the pizza.

"I never ever want to talk about tonight," Jonnie said. "I do not want to remember it either. I saw our whole future vanish when the truck headed for that door. I do not know how it stopped. If Mr St Clare ever asks for another favour you better not agree to do it. From now on we are the most honest people in the country."

Marty knew better than to say anything. They rode around until Jonnie was exhausted then finally went back to the clubhouse.

The next morning Marty had a hard time waking Jonnie. Normally he would let him sleep but there was a gaping hole in the downstairs floor. They had to replace the planks before someone arrived.

Finally Jonnie realized he had to help because Marty could not move the planks on his own.

They got the planks in place then Jonnie moaned.

"What is wrong?" Marty asked. "Did you hurt your back?"

"No, nothing like that. Look at the floor."

There were heavy black tyre marks where the truck wheels had spun.

"We will never be able to clean them off," Jonnie said. "What are we going to do?"

"Don't worry about it. I will take care of it, you go back to bed."

Jonnie did not argue. Marty knew he could not use water so he went to the hardware to get some degreaser. He worked as fast as he could because he was afraid the girls or Mr Wilson would come by.

The degreaser worked but it left a clean spot on the floor. Marty went into the lane and scooped up some fine dirt then sprinkled it on the floor. He was pleased with the results. He rummaged around it the kitchen and found enough to make breakfast for them. They were eating when the girls arrived.

"We came by to have breakfast with you," Sharon said. "Looks like we are too late."

"We will go to the café and have coffee with you," Marty said.

They sat in the café and talked.

"My parents are arriving this afternoon," Gloria said.

"My mother is coming tomorrow afternoon," Jonnie replied.

"This is it," Marty said, "the end of our old life. We will graduate, then have a party and start our new life next week in a new house. We did it."

"We start our jobs next week too," Gloria added.

"You all have something to do except me," Sharon said. "I do not have a job.

"You are going to be our secretary," Marty said.

"Big deal. All I will do is sit alone all day waiting for the phone to ring."

"You can go around with Mr Wilson and me while we look for properties to buy," Marty said.

"That will be better than sitting around all day."

"Speaking of Mr Wilson," Jonnie said, "we have not seen him since exams have started. We should visit him. He will think we have abandoned him."

"You boys go," Gloria said. "I have to get ready to meet my parents. I will see you at graduation practice tomorrow morning."

"I will go with you," Sharon said. "See you tomorrow Jonnie."

"That was strange," Jonnie said. "What is wrong with the girls?"

"They just realized their old life was over," Marty said. "They are shocked."

"I suppose we are too, I hope they recover quickly."

"The graduation will wake them up," Marty said. "Come on, I bet Mr Wilson is wondering what happened to us."

The boys were surprised when they went into the house. It was a mess. They knocked on Harold's door and heard a moan. His apartment was worse than the parlour. A moan came from the bedroom. They cautiously looked in and saw Harold lying face down on the bed. He was naked. The room was a mess and it smelled of stale urine.

"Mr Wilson, what happened to you?" Jonnie asked.

Harold lifted his head and moaned. Then he said, "Hello, Jonnie, am I glad to see you."

Marty and Jonnie turned him over. He moaned as he was moved. He was filthy, dirty and had not shaved for days.

They propped him up so he could speak. "I slipped coming out of the shower and fell and hurt my back. It took me all day to crawl to the bed."

He had difficulty speaking and his voice was harsh and dry..

"Marty, get him a drink of water," Jonnie said as he tried to make Harold comfortable.

Harold drank the whole glass then asked for another one. When he composed himself he told them what happened. "I got up and had a shower, then I was going to come and look for you guys but I slipped getting out of the tub and fell and hurt my back. It took me all day to crawl to the bed. I do not know how long

I slept but it took a long time to get to the toilet and back. I do not know how long I have been like this."

"Mr Wilson, when did this happen?" Jonnie asked.

"It was Saturday. I knew you had finished exams so I was going to drop by for a visit."

"Saturday," Marty exclaimed. "It is Wednesday. You have been laid up for five days. Have you had anything to eat?'

"No, I have been confined to this bed. Five days, that is hard to believe. I am hungry."

"Mr Wilson, you are in a bad way," Jonnie said. "I am going to call an ambulance. You should be in the hospital."

"I will be all right now that you boys are here. I am hungry, get me a bowl of cereal. I will be all right."

Jonnie went into the kitchen to get the cereal but the milk had gone bad. He found a tin of chicken soup and warmed it.

"Eat this, then we will get you cleaned up and then you can have a real breakfast,"

The soup revived Harold so the boys tried to figure out how to get him into the shower.

"The lady next door has a wheelchair, it belonged to her husband. You can wheel me into the shower."

"You cannot climb into the bath," Jonnie said. "How are you going to take a shower?"

"There is a proper shower in the laundry room. I can shower there."

Jonnie went next door for the wheelchair and Marty rearranged the laundry so the wheelchair would fit, He found a stool for the shower.

Marty watched Harold in the shower while Jonnie stripped the bed and cleaned up the room. Jonnie went to the corner shop for some milk to make Harold something to eat. Marty wheeled him up to the table for scrambled eggs and toast.

"I am hungry, I need more than that."

"We will feed you again later. If you eat too much you will get cramps."

Harold felt better. He could sit in the wheelchair, but when he tried to move the pain would stop him.

"You should see a doctor," Jonnie said. "You could have broken something."

"I am all right. I have had bad backs before, the pain will go away in a few days. All I need is rest.."

They talked for a few minutes then Harold said he was tired so the boys put him in bed.

"We cannot leave you alone," Jonnie said, "so Marty and I will move in now instead of next week so we can take care of you."

"That is very kind of you, but I will be all right on my own as long as you stop by to check on me."

"We might as well move now," Marty said. "We have all afternoon as long as we can use your truck."

"I have my license," Jonnie said. "I have driven that truck lots of times, it will not take long."

"I am too tired to argue. Go ahead, the keys are in my pants pocket."

"We have to stop at the service station for some P plate tags," Jonnie said, "then get some boxes at the hardware."

While they were at the hardware Marty gathered some boxes and Jonnie told his uncle about Harold.

"I will stop by after work," Freddie said. "If he is hurt bad I will take him to the hospital."

Marty opened the big door then Jonnie drove the truck inside. Marty started to go upstairs, when Jonnie told him they would empty the basement first.

"There is nothing in the basement ,our things are upstairs."

"Have you forgotten the other elephant? We have to move the money too."

"I forgot all about the money. Come on, let's get it before someone comes."

"Lock the door, no one will bother us."

Marty ran up and down the stairs with the money bags while Jonnie packed them in the boxes. He marked each box with a letter to designate what type on note was in it. There were lots of boxes with 'S' on them.

"This is the only time we have to move the money," Jonnie said. "I thought of it while we were talking to Mr Wilson.

They went up to their rooms and tossed their belongings on the bed then wrapped them in the blankets. They took the two white boards, the TV, and desks too. The last thing was the food in the refrigerator. Marty pulled the plug and said, "That is it, we are finished here."

They went downstairs then turned off the electricity and drove away.

"We had a good life there," Jonnie said, "but we are going to have a better one from now on."

They had just finished packing the money boxes in the secret closet when Freddie arrived. He talked with Harold for a while then said he would make an appointment for Harold with his chiropractor for noon tomorrow.

"That is going to be hard for us," Jonnie said. "We have graduation practice in the morning. We may not be here at noon."

"I can get him in the tuck with the wheelchair so don't worry. The missus and I will not be at the graduation but we will come to the party that evening."

Marty helped Jonnie put their clothes away then he went home. Jonnie straightened out the rooms. His mother and Francis would stay in the smaller room. He did not want Francis near the secret room.

Jonnie cooked supper then he and Harold watched television until Harold went to bed then Jonnie trolled the stock market until he fell asleep. Marty found him asleep in the chair when he came by in the morning. They settled Harold then went to school to meet the girls and practice. It did not take long. They were issued gowns and hats and told what to do then were sent home.

The gang stopped for coffee where Jonnie told the girls about Harold falling in the shower.

Harold was not there when they arrived so they tried on their gowns. Jonnie and Sharon's gowns were too short and Gloria and Marty had to pin theirs up. They were admiring themselves when Harold walked in.

"You are supposed to be in a wheelchair," Sharon exclaimed.

"Where is Uncle Freddie?" Jonnie asked.

"He dropped me off. We had lunch after the chiropractor. I was amazed, he thumped me in the lower back and all the pain went away. I am cured."

"Well, you go slow and heal properly," Jonnie said.

"I have to go," Gloria said, "I am expected for lunch. Marty, you are invited for dinner tonight."

"I am sorry, dear, but my uncle and aunt are here for the graduation. We are going out for supper."

"My mother will be here this afternoon," Jonnie said,

"My family are gathering for the graduation too," Sharon said.

"It is going to be confusing for the next couple of days," Jonnie said. "Let's go along with what our parents want to do then we will meet somewhere afterwards."

They all agreed it was impossible to make any plans until after graduation.

The girls left and Marty went home. Jonny stayed with Harold. He searched the stock market until his mother and Francis arrived.

Jonnie was pleased to see his mother. She looked younger and very happy. Ida was happy to know her son was so well adjusted. She and Francis both liked Harold, especially knowing there was an adult to watch over Jonnie.

They sat in the parlour sipping drinks and catching up. Then Jonnie showed them around the house. They were pleased they did not have to stay at the clubhouse.

When Francis and Ida settled in, Jonnie sat them in front of the Teletext and explained how the stock market worked. They were fascinated and surprised when Jonnie told them he was a trainee stockbroker. Ida was proud of her son.

CHAPTER SIXTEEN

The next morning was just like any morning for the boys, except they were going to school for the last time and their parents were with them.

The graduation was not like the ball they attended last year. Sharon and Jonnie were not the king and queen. This time they were just students standing in line, waiting to be called to receive their diploma. The only exciting part was after the school song when they tossed their caps in the air.

There were the obligatory photographs, then a farewell in the gymnasium.

Francis and Ida were pleasantly surprised when Jonnie introduced Sharon and her family to them. Then Marty came along with his and Gloria's family. After introductions they decided to meet at the Chinese restaurant for a party that evening.

When they broke up the students tossed their gowns and caps in the laundry bins provided and walked out of the building for the last time

The party was a happy affair. The parents were proud of their children and the children were proud of what they had accomplished.

As they were leaving, Sharon's parents invited all of them to their place for a barbeque the next afternoon.

The whole group were worn out the next morning so they relaxed, except Sharon and her parents. They had to prepare for the barbeque.

Jonnie spent the morning searching the stock market. Francis sat watching him. He could not understand how Jonnie could make anything out of all those numbers.

Then Jonnie caught on to some movement. He explained what he was doing. Francis was mesmerized watching him. Finally Jonnie called in his results.

"I just made two thousand dollars for the company," Jonnie said. "I could make more this afternoon but we are going to Sharon's."

Francis could not believe that so much money could be made that easily.

"I could lose that much just as easily," Jonnie answered.

Marty gave his father five dollars to buy some meat for the barbeque and everyone brought something to help out.

Everyone was happy they were celebrating a milestone in their lives. The youngsters had graduated and the parents were proud of their achievements.

They toasted their achievements then enjoyed a friendly afternoon.

When everyone settled down, Sharon's father stood up and spoke. "Thank you all for coming and celebrating with us. We are proud of what our children have achieved but I am sure we parents have only heard partial stories of what the youngsters have planned. I would like each one of them to tell us what their plans for the future are."

The others agreed and lightly applauded.

"Good, let's start with Jonnie. He appears to be the ringleader. Stand up, Jonnie, and tell us your plans for the future."

"Thank you. I am not the leader. We are all in this together. Marty and I realized long ago that we could not find a good paying job like normal people so we decided to start our own business. We took the business course in out last year and plan to go to tech college to learn business procedures. We had planned to start slowly and steadily build up our business. All of that has changed. We met Sharon and Gloria and have included them in our plans. Also we already have a business name, a telephone and an office. Gloria and I start work tomorrow morning in the city. She is going to design clothes for Grace Brothers and I am starting training as a stockbroker. Marty and Sharon are going to the courthouse with Mr Wilson to apply for a real estate licence. They are going to work out of an office in our new home. Mr Wilson is an accountant and we have a lawyer to take care of all our legal matters. We are well ahead of our original plan and I know that we will be successful. Thank you."

"Well, that was a surprise, we did not know you had a business name and an accountant and a lawyer. You have really surprised us. Now, Sharon, would you please tell us your plans?"

"Thank you, Father. The others already know what they are going to do but I have no idea of what I am going to do. We were going to spend the summer getting organized then go to tech but that has all changed. I am going to learn real estate procedures with Mr Wilson and Marty. I may change to something else later but I have to do my share in this enterprise. Jonnie and I are going together and later plan to marry. We realize that we have to work together to be successful and we are going to be successful, thank you."

"Mother and I knew you and Jonnie were going together but we did not realize it was serious. We will do all we can to help you my dear. Now it is time for Gloria to tell us her story."

"You all know I am very good at gymnastics and Marty was coaching me on the trampoline. I had a dream of being a dancer but I realized that would not happen while I was in Tasmania. I had no idea what I was going to do until Marty convinced me to join with the others and go to tech next year to learn business techniques so we all could start a business. My life changed when we went to Grace Brothers on a school excursion. Their head seamstress liked the clothes I was wearing. I had designed them. She asked me to bring in some samples of my designs. When she saw them she asked me if I would join their design team. I start tomorrow designing the teenage fall wardrobe. I never realized my hobby would become my profession. One more thing that has happened. Marty and I are planning to marry when we have settled down and know what we are doing. Right now we are going to live at Mr Wilson's home. Jonnie and Sharon are going to live there too. We have made a great leap forward in our lives. I know we are going to be successful because we all want to be. Thank you."

"Well, that is a real shock," Mr Cloutier said. "Gloria, dear, Mother and I knew you liked Marty but we did not realize you were that serious. We were planning to take you back to Tasmania for the summer. We love you, my dear, and have seen how self-assured and happy you are. Just like all the others here we are proud of you and will support you as much as we can."

"Thank you, Father. Marty and I will come to Tasmania on our honeymoon."

"Well, this is turning out to be a very eventful afternoon," Sharon's father said. "Now it is your turn Marty. You will have to have something spectacular to top the others."

"Thank you, everyone. There isn't much more to say. Jonnie and I have been planning for this for a long time. We were going to spend the summer exploring different ideas and going to tech to learn business procedures. Well, that has all changed. We are still going to tech, but at night because we will all have day jobs. I like real estate. I have been training with a local company and they will take me on as a salesman when I have my licence. Mr Wilson, Mr St Clare and Sharon and I have decided to start our own company. We are pooling our money and buying properties to sell later when the boom starts. The men are putting up the money and Sharon and I are going to manage and sell the properties. Jonnie is already making good money so he will support us until we begin selling. I have a few other ideas that I hope will contribute to our overall plan As Gloria said, we are going to be successful because we want to be and we have to be successful because it is the only way we will have a good life. One more thing. I was going to wait until I sold my first property before I did this but when I told my mother what I was going to do she had a better idea. As all mothers do. Gloria, my dear, will you come here?"

Marty held out his hand for Gloria. She took it and stood beside him.

"My dear, I was going to by a big diamond when I sold my first property but I realize it is not the diamond that has any meaning. It is what we feel for each other. Gloria, I love you with all my being and I want to be your husband. Will you marry me?"

Marty knelt down and looked into Gloria's eyes. She bent over and kissed him. "Let's get married right now," she said with tears running down her cheeks.

"My mother gave me her mother's wedding ring. They had a long and happy marriage. I know we will too."

Marty put the ring on Gloria's finger then they kissed while everyone applauded.

"You did it, Marty, you topped everyone. Congratulations," Sharon's father said. "We are proud parents because we have children to be proud of."

They spent the rest of the afternoon discussing their ideas with their parents. Mr Wilson and Mr St Claire came by and so did Freddie and Martha. They had a light supper then said their goodbyes. This was the end of their student days. Tomorrow morning they would start their adult lives.

CHAPTER SEVENTEEN

Everyone was up early. There was a little confusion as they all tried to get ready at the same time, then they had a quick breakfast together.

Jonnie did not have to leave as early as Gloria, but he did not want her to be on the train by herself. Jonnie arrived early and set to watching the board.

Gloria was warmly greeted on her first day.

Marty and Sharon were waiting for Mr Wilson.

"The courthouse did not open until ten," Harold said, "so why don't we drive around looking for some properties."

They quickly agreed because they did not want to sit around all morning.

"The Saturday paper is the best place to look of properties," Harold said. "I've circled a few good ones."

They were a bit disappointed because they only found one that had some potential. But Sharon had spotted another one with a worn sign on it.

While they were looking at it, Sharon took out a camera and photographed it.

"It looks structurally sound," she said, "and is in a good location. I wonder why no has bought it."

They arrived at the courthouse a few minutes early and sat on the bench outside the clerk's office.

"Harold Wilson, I have not seen you for years," the clerk said when he opened the door. "Come on in."

"Hello, Horace, I thought you retired years ago. Good to see you."

"I will never retire. They'll carry me out one day. What can I do for you and your friends?"

"Sharon, Marty and I want to go into the real estate business. Will you help us?"

"You're giving these youngsters a start. Good for you. Now is the time to get into real estate the city is expanding. Tell me what you have in mind."

Marty explained their plan to Horace. He was impressed with Marty's enthusiasm.

"I'm sure with your enthusiasm and Harold's help you youngsters will be successful. You will need a real estate licence; an auctioneer's permit and a builder's licence, and we might as well toss in a second-hand car licence too. You never know what the future holds, so you should have a pawn broker's licence too."

"Thank you, sir," Marty said, "but do we really need all those licences?"

"Son, you never know what tomorrow will bring. Besides, when the new government comes in they're going to make it a lot harder to get a licence. They may cost a bit to keep but you will have a hard time in the future trying to get one."

"I understand, sir, and thank you for looking out for us."

"I have always helped youngsters to get started. Besides, you are friends of Harold. I can never do enough for him."

It was lunch time when they finished at the courthouse. Sharon's purse was full of licences and rule books. They went into a nearby café for lunch.

"The angels smiled on us today," Harold said as they ate their lunch. "Do you realize we can do anything we want? We can buy and sell anything and even loan money. We could even start a bank. You youngsters have the whole world in front of you."

"I think we'll go slow and test the waters," Marty said.

"The money train waits for no one. We're going to ride it to the end of the line."

"All right," Sharon said, "but no wild decisions. We will agree on everything we do."

"Now you're talking like a real businesswoman."

***

Jonnie was very quiet his first few days at the exchange. The system was very complicated and he had a lot to learn. The exchange was a live, fast moving, surreal being. Jonnie had to understand all of it. There were hundreds and hundreds of companies and the same number of stockbrokers, each with their own way of dealing.

Jonnie could just sit there and read the board and inform the others of the changes, but he wanted to learn the system. He would scan the board occasionally, but most of the time he was absorbing all his brain could hold on how the system worked.

***

Gloria liked her work; it was pleasant and quiet. She was designing the fall and winter teen styles. She would discuss her ideas with the head seamstress, who was pleased with her work.

Gloria soon realized the other designers and artists were not very sociable. At first she thought they would get used to her physical appearance, like the school students did. When that did not happen, she spoke to the seamstress about it.

"What am I doing wrong?" she asked. "The other designers are avoiding me. I'm trying to be friendly with them but they do not respond."

The seamstress smiled. "I thought you understood, they are afraid you are going to take their jobs or steal their designs. Give them time, they'll come around."

"That's silly, we're working together to produce a good product. If we all worked together we could do great things."

"That would be an ideal situation, but they're jealous of their designs and keep them a secret."

"That's foolish. The designs belong to the company not the individual. Come with me, I'm going to put an end to this foolishness."

Before the seamstress could stop her, Gloria was across the room.

"Hi, everyone. We've come over to ask your advice on the new fall wear. We want the best style possible and if we put our heads together we can come up with something spectacular that will beat the competition."

The others were startled but could not protest because the head seamstress was there.

Gloria went from desk to desk looking at their work.

"That's good," she said to one of them. To another she said, "I like that but it will be in the high price range which is good but we will not sell many. If you change the cut and take away the costly embroidery, it will be a big seller."

That started a discussion and before long they were busy going over each other's designs, making small adjustments to improve them. By the end of the day they had a broad idea of the winter wear that they all liked. From then on Gloria was part of the design team. They sold more winterwear that year than any other year.

***

After lunch Harold drove them around looking for more properties to buy.

"I'm really interested in selling cars," Marty said. "Look for a good location."

They found two more houses which Sharon photographed. Marty was disappointed he had not seen a good location for a warehouse. As they headed for home, he spotted something.

"Stop here," he said. "Look at that."

There in front of them was a very large building, three storeys high, with a rusted fence surrounding it and a yard overgrown with weeds and grass.

"This is just what we want," Marty exclaimed. "A big building in a good location."

"It's a rundown shed," Sharon said. "We can find something better than that."

"We have a little time, let's look it over."

They found a hole in the fence then a broken door. Even though the outside was messy, the inside was clean, spacious and sound.

"This is great," Marty said, "just like the clubhouse only bigger. We can display the cars here and work on them in the back, plus we have the upstairs too."

They looked around and Sharon took some photographs. On the way out, Sharon spotted a worn sign with a telephone number on it.

"I'll call that number tomorrow," she said.

They did some grocery shopping on the way home and had supper ready when Jonnie and Gloria came in.

They soon found out that there was a lot more to the real estate business than driving around looking at houses Sharon had to spend days searching for the owners of the houses they found. Then she and Marty asked Marty's real estate friend to help with the purchase.

Meanwhile Horace chased down the owner of the warehouse. The family member who owned it had died and the others knew nothing about it. Harold said he would make all the arrangements if they would sell.

Then Harold contacted his handymen friend. The properties had to be cleaned up before they could be sold.

Then came the matter of money. They all had promised to pool their money but no one had done anything about it. So Harold called Martin for a board meeting. They all met in the dining room for dinner on Saturday night. The girls cooked a roast and the boys helped.

Over dinner they all talked about what they had been doing for the past couple of weeks. When the table was cleared, Sharon laid out all the paperwork for the properties. Then she gave a summary of each one.

There were ten houses and the warehouse. All the paperwork was complete except the warehouse. She needed the money to purchase the houses.

"I understand that you men have promised to put your savings into this venture. I am asking you to give me the money you have promised so we can start our real estate company."

"I commend you for your presentation," Martin said. "I know you will be successful. Now, how much money do you need?"

"Jonnie told me he and Marty have five thousand dollars that you paid them for working for you. Also you said you would match that. How much can you contribute, Mr Wilson?"

"I can match their five thousand easily."

"Thank you, sir, that's a good start but we need a lot more than that if we are going to purchase all these properties."

Marty spoke up and said, "My real estate friend told me we should buy everything we can right now. He said the prices in the city are climbing and it will soon spread to the suburbs."

"I understand that," Martin said, "and I agree. Tell me how much this is going to cost us."

"A couple of houses are on the fringe," Sharon said. "They are cheap at four thousand each. The other eight are all priced about the same, but with a little paint some of them will be worth more."

"If we can hang on to them for a year they will greatly increase in value," Marty injected.

"All right," Martin said, "eight thousand for two of the cheap ones is half of our savings. I estimate the others are about five thousand each because that is the mean price of property in this area. How are you going to purchase forty thousand dollars' worth of property with seven thousand dollars?"

"I am asking you and Mr Wilson to put up the extra money," Sharon said calmly.

Martin had to laugh. "You are on your way to becoming a real estate tycoon with that attitude. I may have a little set aside, but nothing like that amount and I am sure Harold is in the same position. You will have to curb your ambition, miss, and start small."

"I forgot to include the warehouse Marty wants so he can start selling cars. That is twenty thousand more. We have to start big if we ever want to be successful. It will not take us long to double our money and pay you back."

"I admire your enthusiasm, Sharon," Harold said, "but neither Martin nor I will mortgage out homes to fund this venture. You will just have to scale it back."

"I know this sounds foolish," Marty added, "but it is our chance to break into the market. The man at the courthouse said the government was going to tighten the laws soon. We have to act now and this is only the beginning."

"I admire you young people for wanting to succeed but you can only do what you can afford. Remember, I told you the biggest danger is to get into debt. Then you have to work the rest of your life for the bank trying to pay off your debt. Take our advice and start off small. You will live well and free of debt."

Jonnie finally broke into the conversation. "Everyone, I am proud of Sharon and all the work she has done preparing this report. You have to admit she is doing a great job and has convinced me that we have to buy all these properties."

"Don't be silly, Jonnie," Harold said. "You're not thinking rationally because she's your sweetheart."

"Hold on, Harold," Martin said. "Jonnie is a sly character, he has something up his sleeve. All right, Jonnie, we will listen to your suggestion, but we will not let you borrow from your company or anyone else."

"Thank you, Mr St Clare. Marty and I have a solution to this problem, that is if Marty will agree. What about it, Marty?"

"You are mad, Jonnie, but I agree it is the only solution, but they will have to promise to keep it a secret."

"What is all this silly secret business?" Harold said.

"Hold on, Harold, Jonnie is a sly one. He has something up his sleeve. Tell us your secret, Jonnie."

"It mainly concerns you, sir. If you ever tell anyone, Marty and I will have a one way sea voyage. Will you, and the rest of you, solemnly promise never to tell what we tell you?"

"Come on, Jonnie, nothing can be that dramatic."

"Well it is. You have to swear that you will never tell because it concerns your friend, Jonny Rizzoli."

Martin jumped out of his chair, shaking the table as he did. "It was you two," he shouted. "I do not believe it."

"Marty heard the whole thing while he was spying on Jonnie, so we decided to watch the switch from the top of a container. It was exciting when the cops arrived. Marty saw Jonnie hide the briefcase so we picked it up after everyone left. We have enough money to buy all these houses, Marty's warehouse and more."

The others were astounded; they did not understand what this was all about.

Martin sat heavily in the chair and began to laugh. He laughed hard and long. Finally he calmed down. "You guys have amazed me again. I always thought Jonnie was lying so he did not have to pay my enormous fee. This is wonderful."

He started laughing again.

"Jonnie, what's going on?" Sharon asked

"You are now a successful real estate agent, my darling."

They spent the rest of the evening organizing their real estate business. Sharon would organize the paperwork and Harold and Marty would see to the clean-up and repairs. They were not in a hurry to sell any of the properties; they wanted to learn more about the business first.

The receptionist at the real estate agency they were friendly with went on holiday, so Sharon took her place so that she could learn more about running an office.

She bought the properties through their office while she was there.

About a week after she started she was alone in the office during lunch. The proprietor was known for his long lunches.

Sharon had noticed a man looking at the display board in the window. He had come back a couple of times. Finally he came in to inquire about a property. He could not decide on a property at this agency or another one down the street. He asked to see an agent. When Sharon told him he would have to return later, he said he would try the other agency instead.

"I can show you the property now and the agent will be here when we return."

"All right, I like this property better than the other one anyway."

Sharon closed the office and drove the customer to the property and showed him around. She was able to answer all his questions about the property. Finally, the man said he liked it and wanted to buy it. He did not haggle about the price.

When they returned to the office, the proprietor was annoyed that Sharon had left the office unattended. He was about to chastise her when she told him she had sold the property at the listed price.

That night at supper the gang toasted Sharon and praised her for her accomplishment.

Harold and Marty were busy organizing the work crews. They decided to get the good houses ready to rent then fix the others. Marty wanted the garage fixed up too. He was eager to get into the used car business.

Harold knew a mechanic who worked from his home. He could only do one car at the time. When he saw the garage he could not pass up the opportunity to have his own workshop.

Marty and Harold would go to the automobile auctions to learn how to buy cars. Finally they were ready to buy instead of looking. They went to the largest auction in town. While they were looking at the cars the manager announced the auction had to be called off because the auctioneer had been taken ill that morning.

"We cannot find another auctioneer on such short notice," he told the crowd.

Marty ran up to the manager and told him he was an auctioneer.

"I have not conducted an auction before, but I have been here observing and if you coach me I will try."

"I don't know, son, you have to know how to handle the crowd. That takes experience."

"It is either me or you shut down."

"All right, I will stay with you and explain what you have to do."

The announcer explained to the crowd that they had a trainee auctioneer. "Please be patient, he is learning."

The manager read the rules and explained how to bid then said, "Let the auction begin."

"I need a box first," Marty said.

That set the mood for the crowd to accept him.

The first few cars moved slowly. The bids would start low and slowly climb until the people who wanted the car would start to bid against each other. It was slow moving and boring.

"You have to speed things up, son," the manager said. "The crowd is getting impatient."

"All right, I have an idea. Attention, everyone. To speed things up I am suggesting we start the bidding at three hundred and then increase it at fifty a time."

There was a bit of grumbling in the crowd, then Marty said, "You all know these cars are in good condition, nearly new with low mileages. They are worth more than five hundred. I will start at three hundred and if no bids I will drop down. We have to speed things up, agreed? All right, let's go.

"This car is only two years old, owned by a little old lady. It has always been garaged and has only forty-two thousand on the clock. Who will start at three hundred? Thank you, sir. Do I hear three-fifty? Four hundred? Four-fifty? Four-fifty once, twice. Sold. Next item is a new sports car..."

That is how the auction went. Marty sold the cars as fast as he could talk. The quickened pace excited the buyers so they were bidding faster than they could think.

The manager was amazed. The auction usually stopped for a lunch break but Marty continued until all the cars were gone. The lunch break was a half an hour late.

The crowd was happy and excited. The manager was excited too.

"I have never seen anything like what you did, son. You're a natural. You sold every car in record time and for at least a hundred more than they usually go for. I want to hire you as my auctioneer. I hope you will accept my offer"

"Thank you, I will talk it over with my manager."

The crowd hung around for lunch instead of leaving. The manager realized they had money to spend so he asked Marty if he would sell the cars he had ready for next week. Marty agreed.

"Attention, everyone. The auction has gone so well I would like to continue it after the lunch break. I have twenty more cars in the other showroom. They are higher priced prestige models. Give us a few minutes to organize things then you can view them."

The crowd applauded; they were eager to spend their money.

"That was remarkable, Marty," Harold said. "You're a natural."

"I thought I was going to flop at the beginning but when the manager told me to speed things up I did."

"You speeded things up all right. You were so fast I could not get a bid in. We came to buy some cars but I did not get a chance to buy any."

The manager took Marty into the other showroom to look over the cars. They were expensive prestige cars.

"Most of these are repossessions," the manager said. "They have a reserve on them. I cannot sell them under the reserve. So do not lower the bid, pass them in."

The crowd gathered and the manager explained the reserve situation. Marty began the action.

"Here we go, the first item is a near new BMW. The retail price is six thousand, it has a reserve of three thousand five hundred. Thank you, sir do I hear four thousand? Four-five? Five thousand? Four-five once, twice, sold for four-five. You have a bargain, sir. Next car."

So went the auction. Fifteen of the twenty cars sold above the reserve. The other five were passed in. The manager was very happy.

"This is the best auction I have ever had. You got above the average price for all the cars. I made a lot of money today thanks to you. You made a lot of money too. I will have to add it up. Come into my office later and we will settle up and you can tell me if you accept my offer of a full time job as my auctioneer."

Harold and Marty were sitting in the lunchroom having a cold drink.

"You did it again, Marty," Harold said. "You were so fast I did not get in a bid. We come here to buy some cars but we did not get any."

"We got five of them at wholesale prices."

"What are you talking about? You cannot bid, you are the auctioneer and all of the cars went for more than the reserve."

"You forgot about the passed in ones, we will buy them for the reserve."

"Martin was right, you young ones are clever. That is a great idea. We're in the car business."

"What am I going to do about this auctioneer job? I liked selling the cars but I don't want to do it full time."

"Tell him you will only sell cars here once a week. I am sure he will accept that because he does not want any other dealer to hire you."

"You are just as clever as I am, Harold."

A man walked up to them and said, "Congratulations on a successful auction. I understand it is your first one. You are a natural. I am Michael Thornily, the manager of the Provincial Finance and Loan Company. Those were my cars you sold. I want to thank you for getting such a good price for them. Most of the time they go for the reserve."

Michael did not look like a manager; he was young, good looking and was dressed in jeans and a jacket. Marty liked him right away.

"I want to make you an offer. I want you to work for me and sell our company's cars. This place is a racket. My cars sell for the reserve to friends of the auctioneer. I was thinking of taking my cars somewhere else but the same thing happens and there is nothing I can do about it. I am bound by law to only sell the car for what is owed on it plus expenses."

"These went for more than the reserve," Marty said. "What do you do with the extra money?"

"That's why we auction them. If the public pay more, that is up to them. The problem is we are at the mercy of the auctioneer."

"The manager here has offered me a full time job here. I could sell your cars for you too."

"You would soon be forced to go along with the dealers. No matter where I take the cars the same thing happens. It will be expensive to set up my own yard but I will get more money for my cars. Will you help me?"

"I do not want to be threatened by crooks. I doubt if you could protect me from them."

"I understand, I would do my best to protect you, but they would find a way to get to you. Well, it was a good idea. If you think of a better one let me know."

"I have thought of a better one already," Marty said. "Do you have to auction your cars?"

"No, we have to sell them at the residual on them. I know what you are thinking. Run them though a car yard. It has been tried before; the government inspectors are soon looking into their books. None of the money can go back to our company."

"Mr Thornily, my manager and I came here today to buy some cars to sell in our yard. What if we turned our yard into a storage yard for your cars?"

"I do not understand. What good that would do? They still have to be sold at the reserve price."

"We sell your cars on to dealers at the reserve price plus expenses. As long as the expenses are not excessive no one will mind."

"How are we going to make any money doing it that way?"

"Transport fees, mechanic fees, detail fees, storage, insurance, security and who knows what other fees we can add on. The list is endless. They will inspect us then leave us alone."

"I like the idea but it is still a car yard with signs and lights. They will not let you get away with that scam."

"It is not a car yard, it is a large warehouse with no signs."

Michael stared into space for a moment then his face turned into a big smile. "A warehouse, that is brilliant. Why didn't I think of that? Can I see it? I want to get an idea of the operation. You are a genius."

"That is what I tell everyone," Harold said. "We have to settle up here then you can look at our warehouse."

The office was full. People were paying for their cars and registering them. Marty and Harold were watching how the procedure went. Harold wandered over to the registration desk to watch and pick up some pamphlets. Finally the manager had time for Marty.

"You are a very rich young man," he said. "You sold forty five cars. Your fee is twenty dollars a car. That is nine hundred dollars. You did so well I am going to give you a hundred dollar bonus. I bet you never made a thousand dollars in one day before. There is lots more for you if you will join up with me."

"Thank you, sir, for being generous. I have thought over your offer. I have a real estate business that takes up all my time."

"You are rather young to be a real estate agent; you have taken on a lot for one so young."

"I have a good manager and advisor. We came here to buy a nice car for our business. I just thought I would help you out, that's all. I am more interested in selling houses than cars."

"He was so fast I did not get a chance to bid," Harold said.

"I am sorry to hear that son but I wish you every success in your real estate business."

Michael walked around the large open room looking at everything. He explored everywhere. Finally he said, "This is a perfect set up. We store the cars in here, the mechanic checks them over, then they are detailed and put on show in the other room. Wonderful, it will work. We have a winner here. Most of the cars do not need any more than a wipe down. Finally I have beaten the greedy auctioneers. I have to talk it over with my partner. We will meet you here tomorrow afternoon and make the final arrangements. I am really happy about this."

On the way home they stopped at a pizza parlour and ordered four big pizzas, garlic bread and drinks. Harold stopped for a bottle of champagne. They called Martin St Clare to invite him to the big party that night. They had a good time. Harold described in great detail how Marty sold the cars.

"He was so fast I could not get in a bid," he joked.

"I wish I could have been there to watch you," Gloria said, as she hung on to every word Harold spoke.

Just before Martin left he took Marty aside. "I will be there tomorrow to make sure you are not cheated."

"Why would Mr Thornily try to put something over us? He is the winner in this deal."

"I am not worried about Michael, it is his partner I am worried about. I can handle him so I will be there for moral support."

"Is everything in this city like this? There must be some honest people doing business in the city."

"There are but they are controlled by the dishonest ones. That is how we lawyers stay in business. Good night, Marty."

***

Gloria and Jonnie took the train to the city every morning. Jonnie did not have to go to work that early but he did not mind because he could troll the board without any interference.

He'd noticed something the night before and wanted to check it. When Peter Harvey came in Jonnie said to him, "Mr Harvey, one of our best companies is on the move. I detected a sale of ten thousand shares last night and another of twenty-five thousand shares this morning."

"That is interesting, Jonnie, no one sells their shares in that company. They are blue chip. I will call Harry."

A few minutes later, Jonnie said, "There goes another twenty thousand shares. They were not snapped up like the others. Only a few thousand at a time."

Then Harry called to say, "Three of the top executives have dumped their shares. There is a rumour that the company is being taken over by raiders. We'd better dump our package right now."

"Good idea. Try not to spook the market. Jonathon, you did it again. You saved us thousands of dollars. You are a whizz."

***

Marty spent the morning with Sharon at the real estate office.

"We do not need an office," Sharon said. "Since I showed that house the manager is pleased with me. He said I can sell the next one on my own for the experience. After that I can sell our houses from there too."

"That is a good idea. Mr Wilson and I are busy with the work crews and the car yard so you can stay here. I will help you when I can."

"I thought I would be bored when I started here but this is interesting work and I am learning something new every day."

"Why don't you come with Mr Wilson and me this afternoon and meet the managers of the loan company?"

Sharon had only seen the warehouse when it was empty. She was impressed when she looked around. The mechanic had a couple of his own cars in the workshop and the detailer was doing private work too.

"You are already busy," Sharon said. "When are the other cars coming?"

"That is what we are going to discuss this afternoon. I think they will arrive over the weekend."

Mr St Clare came in and looked around. "This is better than I thought it would be. I spoke to a friend in the motor registry this morning. You will not be bothered by inspectors as long as you do not advertise. So you can get a good price for your cars."

"How can we sell cars if we do not advertise?. Marty asked.

"The word will soon spread though the dealers. There are a lot of car yards in the country."

"What do you mean by that?" Harold asked.

"You will soon be selling cars all over the country. Dealers are always looking for good cars at a fair price."

Mr Thornily and another man slowly walked through the warehouse looking around.

"Mr St Clare, what are you doing here?" Mr Thornily asked.

"Hello, Michael. Jonny and I have an interest in this enterprise. I have put a lot of money into it so I am looking after my interest."

"That is great. Now Jonny will go along with it knowing you are looking after things."

When Marty saw the other man he froze. It was Jonny Rizzoli, the gangster he stole the briefcase from. He tried to look calm but he was shaking inside.

Jonny Rizzoli walked around casually looking at everything. Marty tried to keep as far away from him as he could.

Jonny walked back to the others and said to Michael, "Why did you want to bring your cars here? Put them to my yard then we keep all the money and not share it with these others."

"Jonny, I explained it to you before, we cannot sell the reposed cars to the public. You explain it to him, Mr St Clare."

"Jonny, the law is very strict. If you sell the cars they must have a 'Reprocessed' sign on them and a legal paper setting out the facts and price of the sale. It has been proven in the past that people will not buy cars that way. You will lose a lot of money trying that."

"What is the difference? The cars are going to be sold by these guys and they are going to take all the profit."

"Jonny, leave the selling of the cars to the experts, you will get your share of the profits."

"What experts? A little runt, a gawky girl and an old man. What do they know about selling cars?"

"They know more than you do," Martin said. "Come over here and meet my friends. Jonny Rizzoli, this is my old friend Harold Wilson, he is a lawyer and retired banker. This gawky lady is Sharon Quigley, she is a successful real estate agent. Now here is the brains behind this project, Martin McAlister. He thought up this idea and is the owner of this building.'

"He is just a kid and a runt of a kid, he couldn't think of anything."

"Rizzoli, Rizzoli. Where have I heard that name before?" Marty said. "I know, Mr St Clare told me about you. He won a big court case. You're a gangster."

"Come on, kid, I am a businessman not a gangster."

"You called me a runt, I can call you a gangster. Look at me, Mr Rizzoli. I am not normal. I have to be clever to survive. This venture is my main business deal I cannot get a regular job so I have to work for myself. I do not want you as a partner because you will try to order me around and bring in your stolen cars for me to dispose for you. My only chance to succeed in this world is my dealer's licence. If I lose that I will never have another job and have to survive on welfare and work in a sheltered workshop. I have a girlfriend and we are soon to be married. I have to provide for her. This will be an honest business. No one will be able to say we deal in stolen cars. Now go away and leave us alone."

Marty was standing on his toes looking straight up at Jonny. His eyes were bulging and he was shaking his hand at him.

Jonny stepped back and Mr St Clare moved beside Marty just in case.

"Hey, kid, I am sorry," Jonny exclaimed. "I did not mean anything by calling you a runt. I had a hard life too. I understand how you feel. Since my court case I have become an honest businessman. I am sorry, will you forgive me? We have to get along if this business is going to be successful."

Jonny stepped forward and held out his hand. Marty hesitated slightly then shook it. Everyone sighed with relief.

"Well, let's move on," Michael Thornily said. "We have a lot to discuss this afternoon."

After a lengthy discussion they worked out a system for running the cars through the warehouse. They were tired when they finished because there was no place to sit.

Marty and Jonny realized they had to work together and had discussed a couple of ideas on the running of the business. On the way out Jonny said to Marty, "Marty do you think we are going to make any money with this operation? It seems like a lot of work for very little return."

"Jonny this is a goldmine. We are going to clear four to five hundred dollars on each car that runs through here."

"Do you really think so? That is hard to believe."

"The average car is only half paid for. That leaves about fifteen hundred owing on it. Take away the repossession costs there is about a thousand left. A dealer is happy to make four to five hundred so we split the difference with the dealer, about five hundred."

Jonny thought for a minute then said, "Mike turns over about fifty cars a month, that is two and a half grand a month. You are right, it is a gold mine."

"We take out the cost to run this place and split the rest. I figure we make a thousand each a month."

"Wait a minute, we are supplying the cars, we should get more."

"How much were you making at the auctions? Don't be greedy, Jonny, accept it and we are all happy."

Jonny thought for a minute then said, "Mike was right, you are a clever kid."

The others waited for them to catch up and Jonny said to Mike, "I have been talking with the genius, we are going to make a lot of money here."

"I told you that yesterday, I thought you blew it when you called Marty a runt."

"You got it wrong, Marty and I are pals."

The others laughed and were relieved.

When Michael and Jonny left Martin said, "That was hard work, I have worked up an appetite. Lunch is on me."

They went Martin's favourite restaurant and talked about the new business.

"You did it again, Marty," Martin said. "The car warehouse is a gold mine and all we have to do is stand on the side-line and watch the money come in."

"I am proud of the way Marty stood up to Mr Rizzoli," Sharon said. "You were brave, Marty."

"I had to fight for our future."

"You did the right thing, son," Martin said. "Jonny told me he would go straight but getting rid of stolen cars would be a big temptation."

After Martin left Sharon said, "What are we going to do for the rest of the day?'

"I am going to take the weekend off," Harold said. "I am not as energetic as you youngsters."

"That is a good idea," Marty replied. "We are big businesspeople now, let's enjoy it."